So Amazing

by

Sinclair LeBeau

Genesis Press
Indigo

Indigo is an imprint of
Genesis Press, Inc.
315 3rd Ave. N.
Columbus, MS 39701

So Amazing

ISBN: 1-58571-038-5

Manufactured in the United States

First Edition

To my husband, Edward James,
and my children, Ted, Kevin and Kimberly.
Thanks for all your love and support,
and
in loving memory to the best friend I've ever had,
my mother, Rosa

Other titles by Sinclair LeBeau:

Glory of Love (Indigo)
Somebody's Someone (Indigo)

Chapter 1

The elevator doors opened with a sucking hiss on the fifth floor of the Chadwick Building in Harper Falls, Virginia. Jenny Martin felt her stomach lurch, experiencing the familiar pangs of her insecurities. That feeling of not being bright enough, attractive enough—and on and on. These doubts were her constant companions. She clenched her teeth and tried to shake off her doubts. Hadn't she survived Earl's abuse? And there was her daughter to think about. A new life for them. Freedom.

Jenny inhaled deeply, then exhaled to ease her tension and to calm the I can't do this demon hidden deep within her. Still standing in the elevator, she kept one hand positioned on the door, considering a quick getaway. She gulped and stared at the bold lettering that adorned the office door that faced her. L. Strong Architectural Firm, Inc. She contemplated not going on with this interview. It had given her nightmares ever since her friends, Addison and Nina Wagner, both doctors, had arranged it and urged her here.

Was she really capable enough to work for someone like this Laurence Strong? She, who had passively suffered Earl's savage beatings and had come to see herself as worthless. Would she cringe or scurry away like a frightened rabbit the first time one of Strong's clients frowned at her? She had read the recent *Ebony Magazine* article on him several times. She had been impressed by the stylish pictures of him, posing at his office located in Chicago and at the sites of the outstanding structures and lavish homes he had designed. Words like brilliant, creative, and amazing were used by the journalist who described his skills as an architect. Coming face to face with him on her own was intimidating. Why in the world had she let her friends persuade her into thinking she had a chance to work in Mr. Strong's office as an office assistant? She was a woman who had come from the "School of Hard Knocks." How would she be able to deal with the influential clients who would frequent this business dynamo's office?

But Jenny knew she couldn't afford to be scared. She was on her own now that Nina and Addison had moved to Chicago. And she had a seven-year-old daughter to take care of. With this thought, Jenny released the door to the elevator. She needed a good job. She had dreams for herself. She wanted to go on to college and one day have a decent career that she could be proud of. Most importantly, she wanted to set a good example for her little girl. She didn't want her daughter to always remember the bad things that they had been through. She wanted Chloe to see that women—especially her own mother—could be independent and successful. She certainly didn't want her daughter to make the same mistakes she had by dropping out of school. With Chloe's interest at heart, Jenny screwed up her courage and pushed open the office door.

Entering the office suite, she was impressed by the spacious reception area. The carpeted space was cluttered by framed pictures leaning against the wall around the room amidst a disarray of several boxes large and small, sealed and unsealed; and there was an absence of any furniture. She noticed that there were other doors that led to other rooms. No one came to greet her. She glanced at her watch to check her time. It was exactly ten o'clock. The time that she had been told to arrive. She felt slighted. She figured that they didn't think enough of her to have someone there to meet her at the specified time for this job interview. She jumped in alarm when she heard the voice of an irate man. The booming voice vibrated throughout the deserted office. She quivered in fear. Surely that harsh tone didn't belong to Laurence Strong.

Stepping to the middle of the reception area, she peered through the open doors that led to a hallway and to several other rooms. She recognized Laurence Strong at once. However, he wasn't the cool, sophisticated man she remembered from the glossy pages of the magazine. This man was a tall, frighteningly powerful-looking man. Jenny's breath grew short, knowing she had come to be interviewed by this person.

"Like hell, you will!" Mr. Strong ranted into his cellular phone. "I demand that you straighten out that piece of crap damn quick. I refuse to have my name and reputation put on the line because of your f*#*#*g incompetence!"

Listening to the blend of impatience and the degree of anger in his voice, Jenny's lips quivered. Was she strong enough yet to deal with a man like him? He could unravel the fragile control and self-assurance that had taken her nearly two years to achieve after Earl's imprisonment.

Nearly paralyzed by fear, Jenny considered dashing for the door. Then Laurence Strong turned and glared over his shoulder at her. "Yes!" he barked.

Trembling on the inside, Jenny offered him a too-bright smile. She had always used her smile to shield her true feelings from a world that had given her nothing but heartache, disappointment, and loneliness for most of her life. "I'm Jenny Martin. I came about the job," she replied in a tentative tone.

Laurence Strong excused himself from his phone conversation and covered the receiver with his hand. "I'll be with you in a minute." He attempted a smile. He shifted his gaze from her and renewed his conversation. "Don't be such a punk. You've got to kick some ass. If you don't have the balls to do it, I'll be glad to do it royally. I refuse to be f#*#*d with," he growled. Then he lowered his voice and spewed out more obscenities and threats.

Filled with terror from what she had overheard, Jenny inched toward the door, clutching her purse to her chest to ease the thumping of her heart. She felt as if she were "Little Red Riding Hood," about to be attacked by the "Big Bad Wolf." She was anxious to get on with the interview, so she could get away from this man; his behavior reminded her too much of her ex-husband, Earl. Listening to the Strong guy raving, she closed her eyes as if she could block out the sound. It didn't help. Behind her closed eyes, she saw the image of Earl, hovering over her, arguing over next to nothing. She gulped at the awful memories: he would always vent his anger by knocking her around as if she were a rag doll. Jenny shivered with fear; she shook her head to rid herself of the ugly memory. Regardless of the pay, maybe this job wasn't worth it. Did she have the kind of strength or courage to deal with a man like this Laurence Strong, if he was going to be as exasperating as she had witnessed?

The article on him had been misleading. She had been led to think that he was this cordial and laid-back kind of guy. A man who would be a dream to work for. Obviously, he had been on his best behavior for the interview, she thought bitterly.

Laurence Strong strode into the reception area, wiping perspiration from his furrowed brow with a handkerchief. He looked at Jenny as if she were a chore he chose not to be bothered by at the moment. He took a deep breath, studying her face while forcing a smile. "Ms. Martin, is it? You're here about the job." He shoved out his hand in a rote manner. "I appreciate you coming for this inter-view. I really need some help badly."

Jenny accepted his hand shyly and shook it, regretting that her palm was sweaty. His action took her by surprise. After hearing him curse out his phone party, she had expected him to cancel the interview. She was pleased by his firm hand-shake and the way his face had relaxed into a warm expression that made her feel comfortable enough to endure the situation. She decided she had been wrong to take personally his words which hadn't been directed at her.

"We're going to have to talk in here," Mr. Strong said. "As you can see, the place is a wreck and I haven't received any furniture yet. It's being shipped," he explained. "Just take a seat on any box." He settled his long form on a carton across from the one she had taken, which was closest to the door she had entered.

The light blue T-shirt style dress that Jenny had chosen to wear was short and clung to her voluptuous figure. When she sat, the skirt of her dress rode midway up her thighs. She tugged it over her knees so not too much of her café au lait skin would show. With a trembling hand, she touched her glossy, wavy brown hair. For a moment, she wished she had worn the drab two-piece navy outfit that Nina had suggested in their long-distance call the night before. She caught Mr. Strong's eyes as they skimmed her legs with a glimmer of appreciation.

Mr. Strong cleared his throat as though he needed to clear his mind. "Addison mentioned that you are divorced."

"Yes, I am," she responded, wondering why his first question had been a personal one. She watched him doodling on his pad and looking nervous. He rubbed his finger around his collar as though it irritated him. His actions relaxed her. She realized that this man whom she had considered perfect was no different from any other man who had horny thoughts. "I'm a single parent," she added. "I have a seven-year-old daughter who is growing like a weed."

He cleared his throat once more. "Addison has given me a little of your work background. He has

told me that you're working in one of the department stores in town. I hope you have more skills
than operating a cash register," he said tersely.

Jenny tensed at his tone and the patronizing
look he had given her. Her work experience was
limited. "Well, I was a cashier. Recently, I was
transferred to the Customer Service Desk," she
said timidly, as though her minimum-wage job was
something to be ashamed of. Her move to Customer
Service had been a move that she usually spoke of
with pride to her peers. But the mask-of-stone
expression that Mr. Strong assumed only made her
feel more inadequate than she already did.

Laurence Strong gazed at her with a bland half
smile. "Addison mentioned you had some experience with computers, and that you have even taken
some computer courses."

Jenny's nerves tensed even more at his con-
densing attitude. "Well...I'm attending Harper Falls
Community College to learn the basic computer
programs used in business."

He nodded his approval. "Good. But have you
had any real office experience anywhere?"

Her brow creased with frustration. She wanted
to give this man the right answer. She didn't want
him to think she had lived her life doing nothing. "I
have!" she exclaimed, suddenly remembering. "I did
volunteer work at the Women's Clinic with Nina
and Addison. I answered the telephone, took

appointments, did filing and recorded patient information on the computer."

His somber eyes flickered with approval. "Okay,
now that's what I need to hear. I can work with
that. The job is yours." He gave her a stingy smile.
"I'll be opening this office next month. That will give
you a chance to give notice on your job, won't it?"
He gave her a dispassionate look, waiting for her
response.

Despite her fear of him, she felt a hot and awful
joy. "Of course. Sure, Mr. Strong."

"Good. And I prefer to be called Laurence," he
informed her, allowing his expression to relax a bit.
"Right now I'm in transition. I'll be in and out of
town the next few weeks. I have an office in Chicago
to maintain. Here, I'll only be setting up shop to
handle my business while I deal with my father,
who is ill. He lives here in Harper Falls."

He reached for a silver attache case, which was
nearby. Unfastening the locks on the case, he
retrieved some forms and handed them to Jenny.
"I'm glad you've agreed to work for me. I really don't
have the patience or the time to deal with inter-
viewing anyone else. I was grateful when Addison
recommended you to me." He gave her a no-non-
sense look. "I'm counting on you, Ms. Martin. I'm
willing to pay you twice as much as what you're
making at that department store. I am also offering
the same kind of benefits my employees get in my

Chicago office. That includes a medical and dental plan. I'm sure you'll appreciate that, since you have a child."

Jenny's heart danced with the unbelievable opportunity that was being dropped in her lap. "Oh yes, Mr. Strong. Uh...Laurence," she enthused, feeling self-conscious using his first name as she had been asked to do. She was thrilled that she would be making more money than she ever had made in her twenty-six years. While Laurence fumbled through his papers, Jenny studied the impressive-sized reception area and imagined herself in charge, sitting behind a desk and running Strong's Architectural Firm.

Laurence seemed to be pleased at the look of delight on Jenny's face. "I'm glad that my benefits please you so much. I'm used to working around people who have too much and are always whining for more." He paused pensively. "All right, let's get the paperwork straight on you. I'm going to need you to fill out these forms for my records." He reached in his shirt pocket and handed her a ballpoint pen. "Use one of these boxes as a makeshift desk," he suggested, pointing to a box near her.

Laurence moved from where he sat and strode over to her to hand her the forms.

Jenny accepted them and offered a polite smile. "Thank—"

Impatiently, he held up his hand to halt her comments. "Well, I'll be in touch with you within the week. By then, I'll be able to give you a definite date when to report to work. When you're done, leave those forms there," he instructed in a dismissive tone. "Excuse me, now I have an important call to make." Abruptly, he vanished into the office where she had first seen him.

Laurence Strong was a complex man, she decided. Her first concept of him had been of a gruff and threatening man, but then he had been kind-hearted enough to hire her on her limited experience. At the same time, he had dismissed her in an aloof manner that left her wondering which man she would be working with. She experienced a gamut of perplexing emotions, thinking about what she had observed of his abrasiveness since she had arrived for the interview.

While she filled out the forms, she heard Mr. Strong resume his demanding, belligerent tone; she suddenly wondered if she was really doing the right thing by agreeing to work for him.

Hadn't she vowed not to be controlled by any more domineering, obnoxious men? She tried to tell herself that she was wrong to judge this professional man. Certainly Nina and Addison wouldn't have recommended this job to her if they suspected Mr. Strong would be dreadful to her, she reasoned.

When Jenny finished filling out the forms, she checked them over, then left them on the box as her new boss had instructed. She glanced in the direction where Laurence had closeted himself. She could hear still his tirade.

"Baxter, you dumb-ass bastard, I want you off my job!" he shouted. "You've f#*#*d up this job and damn near ruined me with your incompetence. You'll never work for me or anyone else I know again." He paused. "Damn you! I'll ice-skate in hell before I'd give you a second damn chance to screw me!" Another brief hesitation. "Yeah, yeah...that'll be the day, you bastard. Burn in hell, mother#*#*#*#r!"

Mr. Strong's hostile conversation chilled her. Each of his verbal attacks made her cringe.

She trembled from her ambivalent emotions. She stared at her completed forms, which rested on the box, and considered ripping them up and passing up this great opportunity. But then she told herself his anger had nothing to do with her. She rested her hand on her stomach where nervous butterflies fluttered. The kind of temper Laurence Strong exhibited reminded her of the reasons her marriage had been such a disaster.

Blam! The unexpected noise of his door being slammed caused Jenny to gasp with fear. Grabbing her purse, she scurried out of the office. She inhaled deeply, reaching for tranquility within herself. How silly of her to react this way, she thought. Laurence wasn't talking to her. His anger had nothing to do with her, she reminded herself. Outside the office she stepped to the elevator and punched the button. She would do fine. Yes, she would, she assured herself as the doors to the elevator opened to allow her entrance and a retreat.

Chapter 2

"Ms. Martin, this is not what I requested," Mr. Strong said in a tensely controlled tone. He held out the folder to her and gave her a piercing look. "After a month of working here, I expect better of you."

Jenny stiffened, momentarily abashed. "Sorry, Mr. Strong. I'll get what you need right away." She accepted the incorrect information she had given him and hustled out of his office and to her desk in the reception room. Behind her, she heard the sound of Laurence's and his client's laughter. She wondered if Laurence had made some joke at her expense to distract the client from the delay and her inefficiency. She fumbled through the chaotic mess on her desk for the folder she had held moments before Laurence had requested it. It was difficult for her to keep up with the demands of her workaholic boss. He was capable of handling more than one task at a time. He kept her shifting from one job to another all the while she had to answer the telephone, greet clients and attend to her cor-respondence which had to be done on the comput-er. Gasping with relief at the sight of the right folder, she hurried back to his office and placed the desired folder beside Laurence without saying a word. She didn't want to disturb the discussion he was having with his client, Mr. Grayson.

Laurence flashed a look of impatience and slid the folder in front of him and opened it. "Ms. Martin, you can remove these other files from my desk. I need the space to spread out my blueprints," he instructed her matter-of-factly.

Jenny moved to the side of his desk, where a stack of files was piled high. As she grabbed the folders, they spilled from her arms and knocked over Laurence's cup of coffee. The hot liquid ran over the papers and the blueprints he had reached out to demonstrate.

Laurence bolted out of his seat. "Damn it! Hand me something to wipe this up with! Quick!" he commanded, scowling. He picked up the dripping papers to try to salvage his blueprints.

Terrified, Jenny clutched the remaining folders in her arms and lunged for the tissues on the opposite side of him. When she reached over to sop up the mess, she dropped the stack of folders she had been awkwardly holding on to.

Laurence let out a disgusted groan. "Forget it, Ms. Martin. Just leave. I'll take care of this. Find something else to work on," he snapped.

Feeling humiliated, she hastily gathered up the spilled files and hurried out of the office, closing the door behind her. She leaned against the door and tried to calm her jangled nerves. She had been working for him only a month, but it felt more like a whole year. Whenever she was around Laurence, she became all thumbs. Her boss was impatient—a demanding perfectionist. Whenever he called her name, she knew he expected her to be prepared to deliver whatever information he needed. From the time he burst through the office each day, he had her hopping around to fulfill his wishes—Bring me the blueprints for this project, e-mail this report to my office in Chicago, arrange a conference call for me with these clients within the hour—Jenny often found herself entangled in two or three projects at one time. And much to her dismay, she often botched one of the tasks in some way on her first attempt.

Every day, since she had come to work for Strong Architectural Firm, she had made several mistakes that made her look foolish in Laurence Strong's eyes. Although she liked the prestige of her new job, she found herself yearning for the security and friendship of the people with whom she had worked in the family atmosphere of the department store. Anxiety and fear of Laurence's disapproval constantly stayed with her. But the money and the benefits she had received from her first two checks made her persevere. She kept telling herself that eventually things would fall into place for her. She would prove to this man that she didn't lack intelligence and that she was quite capable of handling any tasks he asked of her.

Busying herself rearranging and filing the folders Laurence had ordered out of sight, Jenny was interrupted by the appearance of a familiar-looking man entering the office. Her heart stood still when she recognized the man as Roscoe Baker. The thirty-something man was of average height and slightly stocky. His medium brown complexion was accented by a neatly trimmed beard. He had been the prosecuting attorney on the case against her ex-husband, Earl. Mr. Baker had been responsible for sending Earl away for the rest of his life. What a bastard he had been during that time, she thought. Certainly, she had been glad that her brutal husband had been sent away not only for his numerous felonies, but also for the trauma he had caused her and their daughter, Chloe. However, Jenny had never forgotten how Roscoe Baker had treated her as though she were trash. Mr. Baker had frightened her; she had even feared that she might serve time, having been married to a drug dealer. Mr. Baker had tried to make her feel worse than she had, because she had put up with Earl's constant mistreatment and run away with her man, deserting her child under duress. Earl had convinced her that they were going to start a new life that would be free of his drug use and any further abuse to her. What a trusting fool she had been in those days, she mused sadly.

She held her breath. Had Mr. Baker shown up on her new job to harass her further? As he approached her desk, she cringed in paranoid fear.

The attorney assessed her thoughtfully. "Roscoe Baker," he announced sardonically. "Laurence is expecting me."

His words siphoned the blood from Jenny's face. She was sure that this man would give her boss all the sordid details of her past. Mr. Strong would have a reason to let her go for sure now. "He's...he's with a...a client...sir."

Mr. Baker nodded. "No problem. I've got time to wait." He turned away from her desk and took a seat across the room. He picked up a magazine and fanned through it randomly.

Jenny sighed. Roscoe Baker was the last person she needed to see today. She had disliked his arrogance, his indifference to her troubled marriage and her criminal of a husband, who had manipulated her into believing he loved her. Irritated by the memories of her unpleasant encounters with Mr. Baker, she swiveled her chair sideways to keep from looking his way.

"Aren't you Mrs. Martin? That Earl Martin's wife?" Mr. Baker asked, frowning as if he were trying to recall details on her.

She cowered from the questions and the association he had made. At first she felt embarrassed
by his recognition, then that emotion was replaced
by annoyance. After all, she hadn't been the one to
break the law. "I'm Jenny Martin," she admitted,
lifting her chin defiantly.

He stared at her incredulously. "So, you're the
young lady Laurence hired." He chuckled and
shook his head. "Lucky you," he said in a conde-
scending tone.

Jenny picked up on Roscoe's insincerity. She
knew that he was good for smiling in one's face
while stabbing a person in the back. He had tricked
her a couple of times, nearly entangling her in her
husband's drug charges. If it hadn't been for the
attorney that her wealthy friends, Nina and
Addison, had hired she could have been sitting in
jail herself.

Stealing sideways glances at Mr. Baker, she
wondered if he would divulge all the personal
details of her past. Things that she was ashamed of
and wanted desperately to place behind her.

Mr. Baker rose from the sofa, walked slowly to
the picture window in the reception area and
glanced out briefly. "How's that little girl of yours?
Have you learned how to be a good mommy?" Then
he moved to stand before her, peering down at her.

Jenny's nose wrinkled in disgust. She felt wary.
The last thing she needed today was to have to deal

with Roscoe Baker. Feeling her fury rise, she rolled her chair back from his intimidating presence. "Do you really give a damn about my child or me?"

Roscoe mocked a flinch and then grinned broadly. "Attitude. Attitude," he chided in a sing-song tone. "I come here and find you in a nice respectable job at my buddy's business and I am impressed. Obviously, you're trying to...to do better and be more than what you come from. Bravo." He clapped softly. "Now you only have to make sure your kid doesn't turn out like her old man." He glared at her.

Filled with fury, Jenny bolted to her feet. She placed her hands on her hips and glowered at the offensive man. "For your information, my daughter is doing fine. Just fine. She's in the second grade and has above-average grades and she loves to draw."

Rubbing his beard, Roscoe smirked. "Swell," he deadpanned. "It's good to know that she isn't a small terror. Yet."

Jenny regarded him bitterly. "I refuse to let her grow up imitating the violence she has seen or to allow herself to be abused. As long as I have breath in my body, she'll have a normal and happy life from now on," she said firmly.

Roscoe studied the rattled woman with a mix-ture of derision and sympathy. "Hey, that's great. I'm always concerned about kids like yours who come from dysfunctional families. A lot of them end up in court eventually, with me sending them to correctional institutions. The last thing I want to see is your kid there in the future."

That remark grated on her nerves. She knew that this man wasn't convinced that she or Chloe were going to make it. She hated the doubt she saw in his beady eyes. "She and I both will be okay. Don't worry about us, Mr. Baker," she hissed.

The door to Laurence's office opened. He came out, leading Mr. Grayson over to Jenny with instructions for an appointment in two weeks.

Laurence saw Roscoe and greeted him with a broad grin. "Roscoe, man, you made it. Come on in," he enthused. He turned to Jenny. "No calls until later. Bring us some paper cups, bottled water and some of those pretzels from the pantry," he ordered, showing Roscoe into his office and closing the door.

Jenny dropped down into her chair and sighed from her stressful encounter with Roscoe Baker. Just as she had gotten the energy to get up to head to the pantry to fulfill Laurence's request, his door opened again. "I hope you haven't forgotten that letter and those reports I asked for earlier today. Once you get those done, you may leave for the day," he said in a cool, businesslike tone.

"You'll have them, sir," she answered quickly.

"Good," Laurence said, closing the door again.

She exhaled and pushed her hair back from her face in frustration. She had completely forgotten about that darn letter and the report he wanted. She had been too upset by the mess she had caused half an hour ago.

Beyond the closed door, Jenny could hear Laurence and Roscoe laughing loudly. Once again, she grew paranoid. She wondered if she and her clumsiness or the fact that Laurence had dared to hire a nobody like her to work for him had been the butt of their amusement.

Jenny sat alone in the reception area and placed the heels of her hands over her eyes. There was a lump of anxiety in her throat. Her eyes burned with tears of humiliation; she wanted to release them but was too proud to do so. This job wasn't turning out the way she had planned. She didn't know if she could withstand the stress of Laurence's temperament and his impatience. She wished that Nina, her personal cheerleader, was in town. Nina had a way of making her look at things from a more positive perspective. She would tell Jenny to hang tough and that things would get better. Jenny had tried hard to do what she believed her friend would want her to do.

But no matter what she did or how she did it, especially when Mr. Strong was around, it always came out wrong. Jenny figured that if he hadn't been so handsome, or as gifted and wealthy as she knew him to be, she probably wouldn't have been such a klutz. In his presence, she always felt as though she wasn't worthy enough to be there working with him.

Jenny heard Laurence's office doorknob rattling the way it did when he opened it to grunt for something. She hurried from her desk and scurried to the small room that was used as a pantry, for the things he had requested. She couldn't bear the thought of Laurence making her look like a simpleton in front of Roscoe Baker.

A few moments later, Jenny tapped gently on Laurence's office door to let him know she was entering. She tiptoed in, carrying a tray with paper cups, two bottles of water and the pretzels.

"Thanks," Laurence said, taking the tray from her and giving her a suspecting look.

She assumed that he thought she was going to repeat the same accident she had caused before. To have him think this way irked her.

Clearly, wanting to end the work day and to spend time alone with his friend over drinks, Laurence said, "I was thinking, Jenny, forget that stuff I asked you to do. It's really not that pressing for today. Go on home. You've had a hectic day. Both of us have, for that matter. Come in early tomorrow, refreshed and prepared to do a better job."

Jenny flashed him a tight, quick smile. "No, I'd rather not leave until I've done my work for the day," she said emphatically. Out of the corner of her eyes, she could see Roscoe watching her with amusement. However, she was determined to show these men that she could handle her responsibilities. The work was going to require her to stay about an hour longer than usual. Mrs. Holland, her neighbor and afterschool baby-sitter for Chloe, would surely accommodate her for that extended amount of time, she thought.

Laurence gave her an aloof look and shrugged. "Suit yourself."

Before Jenny hustled out the door, she glanced at her boss. "If you'd like anything else, just buzz me." She exited and shut the door. Outside, she leaned against the door and sighed from the tension she experienced.

***

After Jenny had left his office, Laurence shook his head at her actions and eyed his friend. "She's more trouble than I bargained for, man," he said in a rueful manner. He opened his desk drawer and pulled out a bottle of gin. "If I didn't value Addison Wagner's friendship, I would have let her go. I only hired her as a favor to him and his wife," he explained to Roscoe.

Roscoe jerked his head in the direction of the door where Jenny had just fled. "Man, when I saw her sitting in your office, I wondered what you were running here. An Outreach Program?" he asked, sipping from the cup into which his friend had just poured gin.

Laurence filled his cup halfway and returned the bottle to his drawer. Then he settled back in his chair and propped his feet up on the corner of his desk. "Hardly. Like I said, I'm only doing a friend a favor. Ms. Martin happens to be a good friend of Addison Wagner's wife."

Roscoe took a swig of his drink. "I see. You realize that your Ms. Martin has a lot of emotional baggage. I prosecuted her ex-husband. I have to give her credit for coming out of that mess she was in with him. Man, she's come a long way from the beat-down-looking babe I remembered. Hey, she's cleaned up rather well. She's quite hot looking now. But I certainly hope you won't try to get next to her."

Laurence shrugged. "Addison did mention something about her having a rough time, but I didn't dig for details. All I was concerned with was whether or not I could get her to work. I don't have time to get involved in other people's dramas. My only concern is her work performance for me. And right now, that is drama enough for both of us." He chuckled, thinking kindly about the daily mishaps, now that the liquor had made him a bit mellow. "And getting close to her is the last thing on my mind, buddy."

"You're a liar. I bet you have had all kinds of fantasies involving her. I haven't forgotten what a lady's man you used to be. But leave that Martin woman alone. She has too many issues, my man," Roscoe warned.

Laurence thought he had done a good job of duping Roscoe into believing he found Jenny unattractive. But he often checked Jenny out when she wasn't aware. Any healthy man would have. The lady had a sexy body. He thought of the way her full breasts had brushed against his arm the other day. Yes, he was a breast man. Standing over her, he had stolen glances of her lovely cleavage. However, looking was the only secret pleasure he intended with her.

Suddenly, the sound of Jenny groaning and weeping distracted Laurence and Roscoe. Laurence jumped from his seat to see what all the commotion was about.

Entering the reception area, Laurence saw Jenny clutching the phone. Her eyes were wide with horror. Tears streamed down her face. "Jenny, what is it?" he asked, placing a comforting hand on her shoulder.

With fearful eyes, she glanced up at him and spoke into the receiver. "I'll...I'll meet you there," she said. "You were right. Thanks so much." Her voice broke. She hung up the phone, then sat trembling and sobbing, her hands over her eyes.

Unnerved by her lost composure, Laurence knelt before her and eased her hands away from her face. "Jenny, talk to me. I want to help you," he said in a calm tone to let her know he was sincere.

Jenny stared at him. Her lips quivered. She could barely speak. "It's my little girl, Chloe. Her baby-sitter just told me that...that a man grabbed her and tried to...tried to..." Jenny broke into a heart-wrenching sob.

Laurence's blood ran cold, thinking of what he imagined to be a mother's nightmare for a young girl. "Roscoe? Get her some water, man!" He took Jenny by the hand. "You must go to her. I'll take you." He stood and pulled her to her feet. Gazing into her eyes, which were pools of grief, Laurence felt a lump of emotion in his throat. "Everything will be all right. I'll be right by your side," he vowed, placing a comforting arm around her shoulder and pulling her to him.

He was unprepared for the glow of warmth that consumed him. The familiar feeling was cozy and comforting. It made him feel ten feet tall to take care of this woman with whom he had been relentless in the last few weeks. He had been in the cold, competitive business world so long that he had nearly forgotten what it was like to help someone in need.

"Here's the water," Roscoe said, offering the cup.

Laurence released Jenny, took the cup and handed it to her. "Take a drink," he encouraged.

Jenny shook her head and glanced at him, giving him a confused look. "No! I...I have to get to the hospital. That's where my baby is." She reached down, grabbed her purse out of her desk drawer, and hustled out the door, leaving Laurence staring in disbelief.

"Roscoe, get the janitor to lock my office for me, man. I'll be in touch later." Laurence strode out of the office to catch up to the troubled woman. Seeing her fall apart the way she had worried him. Suddenly, he felt responsible for her; he wanted to know how things would turn out. He couldn't let her out of his sight in the emotional shape she was in. Catching up to Jenny at the elevator, he realized that he had never really noticed her lovely skin or the way her hoop earrings peeked from under her long wavy hair. Despite the circumstances, his heart quivered delightfully. When he had gotten up that morning and come to work, he had had no idea that Jenny Martin would wiggle her way into his heart and make him yearn to be wherever she was.

Chapter 3

On the ride in Laurence's car to St. Luke's Hospital, Jenny was dazed and petrified. The thought of her little girl possibly being kidnaped or molested by some sick creep turned her wrenching tears of fear into body-shuddering sobs. When Laurence pulled up at a red light, he reached over and touched Jenny on the shoulder. "Jenny, you're not alone. I'm here for you. I'll help you get through this," he reassured her. He handed her his freshly pressed handkerchief. The light turned green and he drove faster than the limit to get the worried mother to her child.

As soon as Laurence pulled up to the emergency entrance of the hospital, Jenny burst from his car without uttering a word or caring whether or not he would linger.

Dashing through the door, she rushed to the front desk, feeling nauseous and weak. The smell of the hospital brought back memories of her bruises and cuts, her black eyes and even broken bones. She remembered the lies she had told on her numerous visits. She had become quite creative in justifying those injuries to keep her husband out of jail. After all, the man who had abused her claimed he loved her and that it would never happen again. All she had to do was to keep everything a secret.

A small-featured black woman, wearing a sweatshirt and jeans, rushed up to Jenny and took her hand. "Thank goodness you're here. They need you to sign papers," Mrs. Holland, Jenny's neighbor, babbled nervously.

Mr. Dwight Holland, a sturdy man, hovered behind his wife. "The whole thing frightened the child more than anything," he said in an assuring tone. "The police nabbed the pervert. I memorized the license plates," he said proudly. "They trailed him up some back road near the railroad tracks. I've identified the creep and he's been arrested."

"I'm grateful for that," Jenny exclaimed, wiping her eyes.

Mrs. Holland took Jenny's hand and gazed at her. "Speak to the doctor, sweetie. Chloe needs you. As far as I can see, your affection will be the best medicine."

Experiencing a tumble of confused thoughts and feelings, Jenny whirled away from the Hollands and stepped up to the reception desk to speak to the clerk. "Chloe Martin. I'm her mother, Jenny Martin." Her voice quivered.

The clerk nodded and turned in her seat toward a nurse who scribbled on a chart. "Judy, this is that little girl's mother."

The nurse set aside her chart. "Follow me, please," she instructed Jenny, leading the way through the doors that led to the examination area.

"Is my daughter all right?" Jenny asked.

The nurse stared at her without giving her an idea of what to expect. "The doctor is with Chloe now." She approached a corner of the room that was curtained off and pulled back the draperies. "Dr. Turner, Chloe's mother is here."

A short Caucasian man with mixed gray hair turned to meet Jenny's look of anxiety. "Mrs. Martin, I'm glad you're here. Your daughter has been asking for you." He stepped aside so Jenny could see Chloe, who had vaulted upright at the sight of her mother.

Chloe's eyes grew wide as saucers; the two plaits she wore had come loose at the ends.

"Mommy!" She reached out to her mother. "I fought him. I kicked. I screamed. I did everything you told me to do if anyone tried to get me," she reported.

"Good! I'm so proud of you. You're so smart." Jenny caressed her daughter's hair and smiled at her to show her admiration. She heaved a sigh of relief. She was glad that she had discussed time and time again with Chloe how to deal with menacing strangers. In the rough areas where they had lived during the course of her marriage, it had been a necessity. And especially when Jenny had

learned of her ex-husband's diabolical plan to sell
Chloe in order to cover a drug debt.

Chloe glanced up at her mother and continued.
"Mr. Holland was in his yard and heard me scream-
ing for help. He ran up to the man with a big stick
and said bad words to him. The man got scared of
Mr. Holland and pushed me into the bushes and
hopped in his car and zoomed off. I fell on some
rocks and scraped my elbow. See?" She bent back
her left arm for her mother to see the large square
bandage that had been applied. "It still stings
some." Chloe poked out her bottom lip and tears
welled in her eyes.

Jenny pulled her scared daughter into her arms
and held her tightly. "It's all over, sweetheart.
You're safe now." She began to cry softly with relief,
knowing her child hadn't been harmed bodily.

The nurse touched Jenny on the shoulder to get
her attention. "I'll stay with Chloe. Dr. Turner
wants to talk with you privately."

Jenny released her child and encouraged her to
lie down on the gurney. "I'll be right back, baby,"
she promised in a comforting tone.

Jenny found Dr. Turner just outside the examination stall. He stepped up to her. "Mrs. Martin,
your daughter's elbow was scraped pretty badly.
We've taken care of that. Otherwise she is okay.
Quite naturally, this was a hair-raising experience
for her. Let's be grateful that things didn't get any

worse," he said in a caring tone. "The next few days, let her talk about this. It will alleviate her fears. She may be anxious and clingy with you. But in time, she'll be fine. She seems like a tough little girl." He opened the chart that was tucked under his arm and began to write. "I'm going to order the nurse to give Chloe something to relax her for the remainder of the day. It will make her drowsy. The rest will be good for her."

"Thank you, Dr. Turner." Jenny managed a weak smile before the doctor turned and directed his attention to the nurse who had eased up beside him to offer him a chart that sent him on his way.

Jenny clasped her hands together and looked upward. She thanked Him with all her heart and returned to the examination stall to get Chloe dressed to take home.

As Jenny exited the emergency room with Chloe clinging to her side, her neighbors rushed up to her. To her surprise, Laurence Strong ambled over to them as well.

At the sight of him, a new and unexpected warmth surged through Jenny. "Mr. Strong, I had no idea you were still here," she said in an appreciative tone. "How kind of you to hang around."

Laurence gave Jenny a modest smile. He squatted to greet Chloe. "How are you, young lady? I'm Laurence Strong. Your mother works for me." He smiled. He eyed the bandage on Chloe's arm and frowned, then muttered clearly enough for Jenny to understand, "damned pervert."

Laurence studied Jenny's red-rimmed eyes, the disheveled appearance of her hair and the nervous way she blinked her eyes. He yearned to ease her stress. But he knew that he was limited in what he could do under the circumstances of the strained relationship they had shared over the last few weeks. Too much at this point would make him appear hypocritical. "You've been through hell, Jenny. You look exhausted. Let me see you ladies home," he suggested in a sympathetic tone.

Jenny's eyes widened. She stared at Laurence as though she couldn't believe what she had heard. Could it be that Laurence was feeling guilty for the way he had been treating her? The sudden kindness of her stern boss was startling. Since she had been working for him, she had assumed he had a heart of stone with ice water running through his veins instead of blood. "Oh, no, I couldn't put you out any more than I already have. Chloe and I can ride home with the Hollands." She met his steady gaze; she was touched by the tender look she saw in his usually cold eyes. She smiled with gratitude.

Jenny swung her gaze away from Laurence to Mr. Holland, who had taken Chloe's hand and was chatting with the little girl. "Please excuse my manners, Mrs. Holland, Mr. Holland. This is my boss, Laurence Strong. He was kind enough to drive me here. I don't know what I would have done without him. He kept me from losing it."

Laurence smiled politely at the senior citizen couple and extended his hand to each of them. "Hello. It's a pleasure to meet you."

"Son, we've heard some wonderful things about you," Edith Holland said. "Jenny showed us that article on you in the *Ebony* magazine. It's great to have a celebrity living right here in Harper Falls."

"And you're such a young man to have accomplished so much," Mr. Holland added. "You're the kind of black man who makes me proud, son."

Jenny noticed that Laurence showed a hint of bashfulness at the older man's compliment.

He uttered a soft thank you, then turned to Jenny and grinned. She liked the look of warmth he lavished upon her. This side of him floored her. Certainly, what she was interpreting was nothing more than his genuine interest in her child's well-being. It certainly wasn't the time or place to determine whether a man like Laurence had found anything amazing in her to interest a successful professional like himself.

Jenny stared at her daughter and palmed the side of her face; she could see that Chloe was getting drowsy from the medication. "We'd better get this young lady home. I feel as though I've lived a lifetime in this last hour," she admitted.

"You're right, dear," Mrs. Holland agreed. "It's been a stressful day for us all." She turned to her husband. "Honey, take Chloe for Jenny."

Without any hesitation, Mr. Holland swooped Chloe into his arms. "Okay, sugar lump, let's go." He headed for the exit with his wife trailing him.

Left alone with Laurence in the hospital corridor, Jenny said, "Thanks again for everything." She heaved an uneasy sigh, considering what she had to ask of him. "I'm going to see how Chloe makes out on the weekend. If she is still anxious, I might have to take Monday off." She slowly turned and headed for the exit to catch up to her neighbors. She waited anxiously for Laurence's response. She didn't know if this would sit well with him now that he had seen that the crisis was over. She braced herself in case he switched back to the irritated persona she was used to at the office.

Falling into step with Jenny, Laurence said, "You do whatever you have to do. I insist. I can handle the office on my own for a day or two. Just give me a call and let me know what you have to do."

Reaching outside, Jenny was refreshed not only by the breezy evening air, but also by the comfort of Laurence's support. His actions during her emergency had erased the memory of the bad temperament he had displayed toward her earlier in the day.

"Well, I have to go. My good neighbors are waiting and I must get Chloe settled," she said, staring up at him with an appreciative smile.

Laurence nodded. "Sure. If you need anything...anything at all, page me or give me a call," he encouraged. Looking into her eyes, he took hold of her elbow and squeezed it. "Take care," he said in a soft, velvety voice. He strolled toward his car on the opposite side of the parking lot.

For a moment, Jenny watched Laurence's tall form sauntering toward his car. Today she had seen a side to him that she liked a lot. It was encouraging to know that he was more than a hard-hearted, arrogant businessman.

***

Leaving the hospital, Laurence considered returning to his office. He had more than enough work to keep him busy until the wee hours of the night. Ordinarily, he would have relished working. But he decided not to hole up in his office on this Friday. Instead, he decided to visit his father. It had been more than a week since he had taken time for a visit.

Laurence was greeted at the door of his father's medium-sized, squarish-framed house by Jeremy Chapman, a live-in male nurse he had hired to attend to his father. Jeremy gave him the black brother's handshake. Jeremy was fifty-two, bald, and a hulking figure of a man who had once been a medic in the Viet Nam War. "What's up, Laurence?"

Laurence stood in the hall and hesitated before going in to see his father. The sight of his dad's failing health always made him feel ill-at-ease. "How is he today? Good mood or bad mood?"

Jeremy met his boss's gaze. "He's been grumpy. He hates that low-fat diet he has to eat. And he's been whining for some hot apple pie with ice cream. He tried to bribe me with money to give it to him. But I refused to give in. I reminded him that he has his doctor's visit next week."

"Good for you, man," Laurence said. Hearing about his father's current mood didn't ease his reluctance to visit him. His father was a proud and stubborn man who didn't like the idea of having his son look after him. "Which room is he in?"

Jeremy led the way down the hall. "He's in the den, watching the sports channel."

Laurence followed Jeremy as though he wanted him to be a buffer to his father, who had a way of always making him feel inadequate.

Jeremy slapped his hands together in good humor. "Yo, Mr. Marvin, we've got company. Your kid is here to see you." He walked over to the older man and touched him on the shoulder. "I'll leave you guys alone so you can visit," he said, disappearing quietly.

Sixty-eight-year-old Marvin Strong sat forward in his leather recliner. On one side of his chair was a clutter of magazines, newspapers and books he had read to while away his time. On the other side, his walker was set beside his chair. He gave his son an expressionless look. "Hey, boy," he uttered without taking his focus off a classic pro basketball game that was being re-broadcast.

Laurence walked over to his father and touched him the same way as Jeremy had. But when he did it, he felt his father's body go rigid from his touch. Hurt by the response, he removed his hand quickly and jammed it in the pocket of his slacks. "How have you been?" he asked in as cordial a tone as he could manage.

Marvin tilted his head up at his only son, his only immediate family. "Fair. Just fair," he grumbled. His speech was slurred and slow. "Don't just stand there. Have a seat."

Laurence dropped onto the sofa and sat on the edge. He eyed his father, feeling a knot of anxiety in his stomach. He still had trouble dealing with his father's condition. It bothered him to see his once vivacious father looking older and weaker. Ever since the awful auto accident that he had been in, the older man had been crippled, and then had suffered a stroke. The doctors had also confided to Laurence that his father had been suffering with depression since his mother had died a couple of

years before. The night of Marvin's accident, he had
been drinking and...driving—returning from a
friend's house on a rainy night. A combination that
appeared to have been a death wish to Laurence.

He shifted his attention away from his father to
the pictures around the room. Most of them were of
the strong man Laurence had known when he was
growing up. Marvin Strong had been considered
one of the best high school basketball coaches in
the region. Though Marvin Strong was a man of
average stature, he had been capable of dealing
with some of the toughest guys who had attended
Harper Falls High School. He had been a mentor to
troubled boys who ordinarily wouldn't have made
plans to leave high school and then attend college.

There were also pictures of Laurence's deceased
older brother, Gary. He had been his father's pride
and joy. Everyone had loved Gary. Laurence had
worshipped his big brother. Gary had been the all-
around athlete his father had trained him to be.
Gary's many trophies for his achievements still
stood proudly here and there about the room,
twenty years after his death. Pictures hung on the
wall, showing Gary's fabulous basketball career in
high school. Gary Strong had been everyone's hero
in Harper Falls, Laurence thought, feeling a tug of
sadness on his heart.

He closed his eyes and tried to will away the
grief that washed through him every time he came

home and sat in this room, which reminded him of a shrine. Having gone with Jenny to the hospital, his mind had been flooded by memories of his own family. He remembered how close and loving they had been before Gary died. While he had waited at St. Luke's for Jenny, he had been haunted by the time that Gary had been rushed to the same hospital and had never left alive.

Laurence could never rid himself of the responsibility of his brother's death. He had been the one driving the car that night. He had been only sixteen, and had had no license and little road experience. Though his father hadn't verbalized it, Laurence knew that his old man blamed him.

Laurence blamed himself, too. His brother's death was a burden that he hadn't been able to forgive himself for. He loved and missed Gary, too. He had been empty ever since fate had parted them. No matter how much success he had achieved or how much money he had made, he hadn't been able to soothe the ache or that void in his life left from the absence of his brother. He owed his success to his brother. He knew that he had always been driven to succeed because he knew his brother wouldn't have had it any other way.

Laurence shifted restlessly on the sofa. He hadn't come to see his old man watch television. He had hoped that just once his father would take the time to really talk to him and show some interest in his life or career. He had thought that returning to Harper Falls to care for his father would change the strained relationship they had had since Gary's death.

"Jeremy tells me you go to the doctor next week," Laurence said.

"Yep. That's right," answered his father. He kept his gaze on the television.

Laurence was tempted to snatch the remote control from his father's hand and turn off the blasted set that always kept them from communicating. He wanted his father to look at him and understand that he still needed him more than ever. In the business world, when you are successful and making money, you still didn't know who really cared for you. While his mother was alive, Laurence had known that he had her love unconditionally. She had been a comfort zone to him. He had hoped to get that same support from his father now that she was gone. "Is there anything you need or want?" he asked, knowing that giving his father things to make him comfortable was the only way he was allowed to show that he cared.

Marvin shifted his gaze to Laurence, then looked away. "Let me see," he said slowly, pursing his lips and growing pensive. Then he let out a low, cynical laugh. "No, son. There's nothing you can give me." His words were spoken in a chilling tone.

Marvin swung his gaze to the picture of his beloved son, Gary. "You've done quite enough, my boy."

Laurence flinched. His father might as well have struck him. If his father had intended to make him feel guilty, he had succeeded. Since his return to Harper Falls, he and his father hadn't had any meaningful conversations. Laurence would show up to see how his father was and dash off with the excuse of business that required his attention. He had done his best to avoid bitter comments like the one his father had made. It was his father who had driven Laurence away from home; he had hidden at college as much as he could. Laurence had graduated college and had begun his career far from Harper Falls, Virginia, settling in Chicago. On the rare occasions that he would come home to visit his mother and was forced to be around his father, he had felt that with each look and word of sarcasm aimed at him his old man was vilifying him for the loss of Gary.

Laurence eased off the sofa and stood. "Well, I won't keep you from your game. I only stopped by to see how you and Jeremy were making out. I'll be in touch," he said. Secretly, he wished that his father would ask him, this time, not to leave but to stay the remainder of the evening.

"Yeah. Okay. Jeremy and I are all right," his father said without even looking his way. "Jeremy is quite a man." He chuckled.

Another stab that diminished Laurence. He had yet to hear his father acknowledge his appreciation to his son for leaving his business in Chicago to come to be near him. Laurence slipped out of the room.

Just as Laurence reached the front door, Jeremy appeared. "Leaving already, man?"

Laurence nodded, beginning to feel smothered with depression from his father's indifference.

Jeremy leaned against the wall. "He's been kind of quiet and sad. He naps in that chair. At night, he talks in his sleep, calling the name Faith." Jeremy paused. "When I check on him through the night, he is tossing in his sleep, moaning Gary's name."

A shiver went down Laurence's spine. His old man was still haunted by the two people he had loved the most, his mother and his brother. Laurence was tormented as well. Yet, he and his father hadn't been able to reach out to each other for comfort, to share their grief. Laurence cleared his throat of the lump of emotion that welled there. "I appreciate the good care you've been giving my father. You don't know how much it means to me. He seems to like you a lot better than me." He laughed nervously at the comment he believed to be true. "You know how to reach me if you need me." He gave Jeremy a good-natured shove on the shoulder and exited the house.

Standing on the porch briefly, Laurence breathed in the warm, summer air. He stared up at the sky, which was spangled with stars. He wondered if his dear mother and brother were looking down on him and his father. He wondered if they thought it was as ridiculous as he did that the two of them couldn't get it together as father and son.

The stars grew blurry from the tears that welled in his eyes from his burden of pain and rejection through the years. He bounded down the steps and toward his car. He thought of Jenny and the spark of coziness that he had experienced when she needed him. It was good to be needed by someone, he thought bitterly. Then returned to the more pleasant thought of Jenny. He wondered how she and her daughter were getting along.

Settling behind the wheel of his BMW, he decided to make a stop at the toy store for her daughter. He could use it as a good excuse for seeing Jenny. Hopefully, the sight of her would lift his spirits, even though he had planned on cheering her daughter and Jenny too with his thoughtfulness. Maybe just for tonight, Jenny, with her tentative smiles, could keep him from feeling as though he was the loneliest man in the world.

Chapter 4

Arriving at 1327 Marple Avenue, Nina's modest sized house and the place she had graciously given to her and Chloe to call home, Jenny found Tamara Petersen, her friend from her women's support group, sitting on her porch, waiting for her return. Tamara told Jenny she had learned of her crisis from a friend who had stopped in at the post office where she worked. She had been so concerned she had rushed straight to Jenny's house without going home to change out of her postal uniform.

Jenny was glad to see her friend. She and Tamara had grown close from their support meetings. She had taken to Tamara, who had managed to maintain a sense of humor and a love for life, despite the fact that her husband had beaten her so badly that her chances of bearing children had been ruined.

After enjoying a delicious dinner prepared for them by Mrs. Holland, Jenny and Tamara sat on the porch in rocking chairs, taking in the comfort of the mild, breezy night.

Tamara said, "I love your neighbors. You are blessed to live close to such good people. That Mrs. Holland is a doll and she is a great cook."

Feeling a bit weary, Jenny folded one leg beneath her and rocked slowly. "They are wonderful. Since Nina and Addison had to leave for those teaching positions in Chicago, the Hollands have been as good as gold to me. And to think I never would have gotten to know them if it hadn't been for Chloe. She's such a friendly child."

Tamara halted her rocker and sat forward. "You have quite a few angels around you. Who would have thought that uptight boss of yours would turn out to be so good to you today?" she said, referring to the incidents Jenny had shared with her.

Jenny chuckled softly. "You really learn who people are when you need them. I had no idea that the man could be so kind. I told you how irritable he can be. I was beginning to think I had made an awful mistake leaving my other job to work for him. I felt as though the pay and the benefits weren't worth the stress he was giving me. And I'd had one of my worst days yet today at work. Everything I touched, I ruined. Whenever Mr. Strong is near me or I have to go to him, I become a nervous wreck." Jenny leaned toward her friend. "I hate that look he gives me when I make a mistake or forget something he has asked me to do. It's as if he's tasting something bitter. It really rattles me, girl."

Tamara grunted. "Don't let an expression keep you from receiving all those marvelous benefits you're getting. You said the man would only be here for a year or two. Shucks! You ought to hang in there until then. Just think of how your association with 'Mr. Big Shot' and his firm will look on a resume when you apply for another job."

Jenny sighed with resignation. "You're right. But until what happened today, I was really thinking of giving up. It's no fun waking up and dreading going to work."

Tamara said, "You're going to be fine. After what I've heard, I don't think you're going to have those problems anymore." Tamara paused uneasily. "Can I ask you something?" she said at last.

"Of course. What's on your conniving mind, my friend?"

Tamara cleared her throat in jest. "I remember that article you showed me, concerning Mr. Strong. The brother is fine and young. A good-looking man like him can shake a woman's confidence. Could it be that you have a teeny crush on him and haven't even admitted it to yourself?"

Tamara's comment caught Jenny off guard; she didn't respond right away. Truth be told, she had certainly found the man attractive. Earl had soured her attitude toward men for a while—so she had thought. Yet, when she was around Laurence she realized that she was very much alive to his manliness. As a young woman, she couldn't help but appreciate his startling great looks, from his piercing tawny eyes to his sensual mouth. He had a wonderful build, which he carried with an aura of sophistication, class and a bit of arrogance. He was the kind of man women dreamed of having.

"I do find him attractive," Jenny admitted reluctantly.

Tamara let out a braying laugh. "I knew it. Oh, this is getting good. I think he could have something going for you, too. After what you've told me, I believe he's basically a good man. He could have easily called a taxi for you or simply closed his door and let you deal with your problems the best way you could. But he took his precious time to make sure you got to the hospital safely. That says a lot about the man."

"Hold on, Tamara. Don't go building a relationship out of one act of kindness. I know I'm certainly not," Jenny said.

Jenny noticed that Tamara's attention was suddenly drawn to the street. "You expecting any company?" her friend asked with a hint of amusement in her voice.

Jenny unfolded her leg and sat upright; she looked toward the street and the car that was parking at the curb in front of her house. The car resembled her boss's, she thought. She jumped to her feet and exclaimed, "Oh, my goodness! That is Mr. Strong."

Tamara stood and leaned on the bannister to check out the man. She chuckled with delight at the fact that Mr. Strong was coming to see Jenny. It only served to prove that there were possible tender feelings brewing between the two.

Glancing down at herself, Jenny wished she had time to change her clothes. Coming home from the hospital, she had put on a faded t-shirt and cut-off jeans that were far too short for him to see her in. She was without a bra as well. He would probably think she was tacky, she thought with a worried frown.

From the darkened porch, she and her friend watched Laurence's tall form exit his car. As he strolled toward her house, Jenny thought he carried himself in an elegant manner, even though he toted a large stuffed animal. Her heart lurched with surprise, guessing that the item was for her daughter.

Tamara elbowed her friend and moaned as though she were tasting something delicious.

"Look at that man," she murmured. "You're going to need your privacy. It's time for me to go home." She dug keys out of her uniform pocket.

The thought of being alone with Laurence at her house unsettled Jenny. "No! Please, don't leave me alone. Yet." Usually, the large amount of work that had to be done at the office kept her from holding any cordial conversation with the man. Up until this time, she and Laurence had been like vinegar and water. What in the world would she find to talk to him about tonight? Her experiences were limited and his were boundless.

Laurence arrived at the bottom of the steps and hesitated. He rested his foot on the first step; he clutched a teddy bear under his arm. "Good evening," he said, addressing both women. "I saw this in a store and thought it might be something Chloe would like, especially after the day she's had." His tone was full of warmth. He hoisted the bear up toward Jenny. The bear was a fuzzy brown with huge, goofy black eyes.

Reaching out to accept the gift, Jenny gushed with appreciation. "Thanks so much! Tamara, isn't he the cutest thing you ever saw?"

Jenny notice that Tamara was busy checking out the man, whose features were made clear by the light that filtered from the open door of her living room.

"Oh yeah, sure. He's simply...adorable," Tamara answered, giving Jenny a look that let her know she wasn't talking about some silly toy.

Jenny caught her friend's sly reference. Embracing the bear with one arm, she reached over and pinched Tamara's arm in jest. "Tamara, this is

Mr. Strong, my boss. Mr. Strong, Tamara Petersen, my good friend."

"How are you?" He smiled. He hoped Jenny would invite him to stay. However, he wasn't in the mood to be charming with her company. Hopefully, her friend would have the courtesy to leave them alone, he mused.

"Come on up and make yourself comfortable," Jenny urged

Ascending the steps, he seemed to be glad that Tamara was descending the steps to leave.

"Nice meeting you," she told Laurence. "I'll call you later, Jenny," she said, walking off to her car.

"Good night," Laurence said, relief tinging his voice. Then he turned apologetically to Jenny. "I didn't mean to run your company away."

"No problem. She was getting ready to leave anyway," Jenny told him. She carefully placed the bear beside one of the rockers and sat down again. She beckoned Laurence to take the seat that Tamara had occupied.

Laurence sat and crossed his long legs. "I'm not going to take up much of your time. I merely wanted to check on Chloe and you. What a day, huh?" His voice was velvet smooth and full of sincerity.

"Oh, yes. But thank goodness the worst part is over. Chloe is resting quietly. She seems to be fine. She wants to return to school. But she wants me to pick her up," Jenny added.

He shifted his body Jenny's way as though he wanted to give her his undivided attention. "Well, it's all right with me if you want to leave work to do that."

"I'd appreciate that. But I'd like for you to extend your understanding a little further."

He studied her face, which was caught by the glow of light that came from inside her house. "What can I do?" he asked in an understanding and friendly tone.

The gentle tone of his voice struck a vibrant chord in her. She could hardly breathe from the tender look on his face. Finding her voice and her courage she asked, "I was wondering if you would allow me to bring Chloe to work."

The request seemed to catch Laurence off guard. Clearly he had expected her to ask something different of him. Money, or perhaps a day or two off. Something he could have given easily. He made a face. Obviously, having a child in his office wasn't appealing to him at all. Jenny knew that his work required a peaceful atmosphere for him to concentrate on the drawing of intricate plans. Although he had been sympathetic to Jenny, concerning Chloe, she suspected that he didn't want to deal with the child underfoot at work.

Laurence's hesitation made Jenny feel ill at ease. Her face fell. Maybe she had asked too much of him, she thought. "If it's a problem," she said quickly, "I'll just have to come up with something else." Her voice sounded hopeless in her own ears.

The helpless tone of her voice and the forlorn expression on her face seemed to cause him to reconsider the issue. He forced a friendly smile. "Sure, you can bring Chloe to the office. I have no problem with it," he said, clearly trying to convince himself that her seven-year-old daughter wouldn't pose a problem in the workplace.

Pleased by his consent, Jenny wanted to hug him to show him how much his understanding and kindness meant to her. Instead, she wrapped her arms around herself and beamed. "Thanks so much," she enthused. "I promise you, you won't even know she is around."

The telephone rang. Jenny jumped to her feet and dashed for it, feeling frustrated that she was being interrupted during her visit with Laurence. "Excuse me," she said, touching him on his shoulder as she left.

Once Jenny had gone inside the house, Laurence rose from the rocker, which he had found uncomfortable for his long legs, to take a seat on the bannister. From where he sat, he had a clear view of Jenny through her living room window. He watched her pace, holding the telephone, chatting and waving her hands animatedly. The sight of her in the t-shirt and cut-off jeans, padding around barefoot, was a sensual delight. The t-shirt clung to her perky breasts and revealed she wore no bra. He could see her swollen nipples. She turned her back to him, shifting her weight to one side, and placed a hand on her hip. His view was now of her curved and rounded bottom and her firm, golden, shapely legs and thighs. Simply divine, he mused. His manly essence came alive as he began to imagine how splendid Jenny would look nude and sprawled upon his bed. He thought of how much he would like to fit himself between those luscious thighs.

Jenny hung up the phone and came back to the porch, breaking Laurence's erotic fantasy.

"I'm sorry about that. It was Nina and Addison," she explained, standing near him. "I'd left a message on their answering machine, concerning Chloe. I knew they would have a fit if they heard about the incident from anyone else. I had to assure them Chloe was okay. They think the world of her," she added.

An awkward silence fell between them.

Laurence studied Jenny, then looked away when she glanced up at him.

"I've been meaning to talk with you," he said. "I have a three-day convention to attend in a couple of weeks in Virginia Beach Friday to Sunday. I'm scheduled to hold several workshops. I had my secretary in Chicago scheduled to work with me on this event. But she has a family emergency that won't allow her to help me. I was wondering if you would be interested in helping me out."

Jenny placed her hand on her chest, clearly agitated. "You want me to go with you? I mean, you'd trust me to assist you?"

He chuckled softly. "I believe it will be a good experience for you. I think you'll do just fine. Of course, I pay all your expenses. We'll have separate rooms," he assured her, so that she wouldn't feel as though he was a lecher.

"I've always wanted to go to Virginia Beach," she said wistfully.

"Well, here's your chance to go. Of course, I won't work you the entire time. You'll have time off to do some sightseeing. School will be closing soon. Right?"

"Yes, it will," she answered.

"The trip will be during the latter part of June. It should fit your schedule with Chloe perfectly. That way you won't have to worry about getting Chloe to and from school."

She rubbed her chin thoughtfully. "I'd like to go. I'd have to make arrangements for someone to keep Chloe. I'm sure the Hollands would be more than happy to look after her for a few days. But I'd have to check with them on their plans. Give me a chance to check with my neighbors. Everything will be dependent on them. I can't go off and leave my daughter with just anyone."

Laurence's eyes were drawn to her figure, especially the way her breasts set up and out and jiggled with her slightest move. "Sure. Sure, I understand," he said, feeling encouraged. He stood up to relieve the ache of his emerging arousal, which grew from his carnal thoughts of her. He jammed his hands in the pockets of his slacks and shifted his posture to tame his body. "It's late and I can imagine that you're more than ready to turn in for the night." He moved toward the steps. He touched her on her arm. "Good-night, Jenny. Sleep tight," he said, descending the stairs.

"Thanks so much for coming by. And I know Chloe will love the teddy bear," she said with warmth. Seeing him stride to the car, she watched him with longing.

She hadn't been ready for him to leave. She had wanted him to stay. His presence was comforting and though she was tired she wasn't ready to go to sleep. She'd seen him checking her out when he thought she wasn't looking. She was flattered. There was a hint of something between them; she couldn't yet pinpoint exactly what it was.

After Laurence had pulled away from the curb, she picked up the teddy bear, hugged it and kissed its funny nose. She wished that she had been able to do the same thing to Laurence.

Wonderful, sweet, kind Laurence. Though the day had begun on an awful note, it had ended filled with more hope than she had known in the last few years.

Chapter 5

Jenny had stayed out of the office longer than the few minutes she had planned. She had slipped across the hall to give Trudy, who worked as a secretary for a dentist, some oversized envelopes until she could get to the office supply store. To Jenny's dismay, Trudy insisted on sharing her plans of her upcoming vacation. Jenny found it difficult to maintain her interest. She prayed that Chloe had minded her and hadn't gone into Laurence's office or wreaked havoc in any other part of the office, for that matter. Her daughter was always fascinated by the man's domain, which was furnished with two drafting tables and all kinds of pens, pencils, rulers and gadgets that he used to sketch and draw blueprints and plans. Chloe also loved to unfurl the rolled designs he kept in a special cubicle in his office. Whenever Laurence left the office for one reason or another, Chloe would beg her mother to show her the designs of the buildings that Laurence kept in careful order in his office.

Jenny smiled tightly at Trudy, rambling on and on about Bermuda, then sneaked a peek at her watch. She was hardly absorbing anything that her friend was saying because she knew she should check on Chloe. Hearing rap music blasting from her office, Jenny groaned. She abruptly ended her conversation with Trudy and hustled into Laurence's office. Chloe wasn't sitting in the reception area, coloring in her books as Jenny had ordered her. Jenny rushed into Laurence's office, feeling panicky.

Chloe sat at one of the drafting tables. Rap music thumped loudly, replacing the soft classical music that Laurence listened to while he worked.

"Chloe Martin! How dare you disobey me," Jenny chided. Her hands went to her face in a rush of panic when she saw several of Laurence's blueprints, unfurled and scattered on the floor. The can of grape soda that Chloe had been drinking had spilled onto the beige carpet near Laurence's desk and one of Laurence's large potted plants had been turned over; a clump of dirt was grounded into the fibers of the rug. "Young lady, you are going to get it," she promised angrily. Laurence would burst a blood vessel in his head if he saw this mess, Jenny thought, dreading his impending appearance.

Chloe stared innocently at her mother; she clutched a piece of red crayon. An elaborate design of a mall lay on Laurence's table with heavy red markings here and there on the blueprint. "I was helping Mr. Strong. These pictures have just lines and no color. I made them prettier. Come see, Mommy." She waved her mother to her.

Jenny marched over to see the damage. She gasped in horror at the color markings her daughter had made with her school crayons. The child's mischievous actions rattled Jenny's nerves. Furious, she gripped Chloe under her arms and lifted her off the stool. The child squealed in fear, recognizing her mother's anger. "You've gotten us both in trouble." She set Chloe on the floor and wagged her finger in her face. "You've ruined Mr. Strong's important papers. And he's not going to like it one bit. Go back to my office, young lady," she ordered. "Sit! And don't touch a thing."

Chloe pouted and scampered out of the office.

Left alone, Jenny stood with her hands on her hips, looking at the mess. How in the world was she going to right this? She had promised her boss that Chloe would be no trouble. But her little girl had made a fool of her.

Whenever Chloe was around, with her constant inquisitive chatter, Laurence would stay in his office, only exiting when he had to confer with Jenny over work he had assigned her. Usually he kept to himself, hovering over his drafting table, measuring lines and sketching structures with concentrated precision. Jenny could sense that his level of tolerance for her daughter had grown thin after the first two days of her presence. Thankfully,

Laurence had been too much of a gentleman to tell
her to make other arrangements for Chloe.

Jenny knew that Laurence had been under a lot
of pressure in the last few weeks, trying to manage
ongoing projects in Chicago as well as beginning
new ones here in Harper Falls. She was so concerned about gathering up the architectural drawings from the floor and re-rolling them, she hadn't
taken the time to turn off the radio, which still
blared rap music. She had just begun to clear away
everything when she saw Laurence looming in the
doorway, a scowl on his face.

He gave Jenny a scorching look. "What in the
hell happened here?" He strode into his office,
snatched the remote control off the corner of the
drafting table and turned off the music. He placed
the remote on his desk and jammed his balled fists
against his hips.

Jenny stared at his irate face and his menacing
pose. The sight of him sent a shiver of fear through
her. His appearance reminded her of the abusive
man who had once controlled her life.

She cowered, remembering the beatings she
had taken. "Chloe. She...uh...I'm sorry, Laurence,"
she said in a small, pleading voice. Still kneeling
from her tasks she curled herself into a tight knot,
bracing herself as though she expected to be hit.

Jenny's diminished figure temporary melted
Laurence's ire. He dropped to his knees and

extended his hand to help her off the floor. He gave her a nervous smile full of concern. "It's fixable," he said in a kindly tone. She had made him feel as though he was a brute with her response.

She breathed with relief and accepted his hand to help her stand. "I went to carry some envelopes to Trudy and got tangled up in one of her long-winded conversations," Jenny explained. "I hadn't planned on leaving Chloe alone for long. But Trudy just went on and..."

To Jenny's dismay, she could see that her nervous babbling annoyed Laurence, who was making an effort to be understanding. He held up his hand to silence her. He seemed to be struggling with his anger. "Okay, I get the picture," he replied curtly. "But I thought we had an agreement. You were supposed to make it clear to Chloe that my office was off limits." He glanced at his drafting table and muttered a few obscenities under his breath. He ripped up the drawing that had been there, which Chloe had ruined. He crumpled it into a ball and flung it into the wastebasket. His jaw worked with barely concealed fury. "What's done is done," he muttered. His expression softened at Jenny's obvious embarrassment. "Don't worry. I have a copy of this." He suddenly fixed Jenny with a piercing stare. "And where is she now?" he asked, scowling again. "She wasn't in the reception room when I came in."

"Oh, my goodness!" Jenny gasped, her hands going to her face. "She had been begging me for some candy. She's probably headed for the snack room down the hall." She rushed past Laurence, nearly causing him to lose his balance.

Laurence heaved a sigh and dropped down on the stool at his drafting table. He sure didn't need this kind of aggravation. He had had no idea what a handful little Chloe could be, when he had first agreed to this arrangement. The child he had seen in the hospital had looked harmless. But Chloe had filled the office with her constant questions, her whining for money to go to the snack machine, and her bouncing up and down on the sofa in the reception room as though it was a trampoline while clients waited there for him. The only time she was quiet was when she was permitted to lie in the middle of the reception floor to draw. He was comforted by the thought that soon school would be closing and she would be in some kind of summer enrichment program and out of his hair. Jenny seemed to feel that by then Chloe could return to her usual routine. The child's fear of that awful rape attempt had abated. Thankfully, the Hollands had agreed to keep her during the summer as they did the regular school year so that her mother could work without having her daughter in the office and Jenny would be able to attend the convention with him.

When Jenny returned to the office, she looked frazzled. "She had bought two candy bars and a can of grape soda by the time I got there. I seized everything. No more sugar for her today. She's been bouncing off the walls from the junk I allowed her to eat earlier today." Jenny set about picking up the remaining blueprints her daughter had scattered. Her eyes were full of anxiety. "You don't have to worry about her for now. She's busy coloring." She looked at him and bit her lip. "Uh...coloring in one of her books."

Laurence stooped to help Jenny clear the floor of his work. The two of them worked in silence until Laurence picked up a couple of drawings that Chloe had left behind. The pictures had been drawn on the office stationery. Studying them with interest, he smiled. Then he offered the work to Jenny. "Looks like you have an artist on your hands." He contemplated a picture of the brown teddy bear with the funny big eyes. It was quite a good caricature for such a young child. He also checked out Chloe's other drawing—a butterfly with eye-catching colors, which was better than the first picture of the bear. Quite impressive, he mused.

Jenny smiled at the colorful renderings her daughter had made. "She loves to draw. She has from the moment she was able to hold a crayon," she explained matter-of-factly.

Laurence stared at Jenny for a moment. How could she have been so naive not to recognize that her kid had artistic potential? "You do realize that Chloe is gifted. This is more than ordinary childhood doodling. She has a mature eye for detail."

Jenny examined the pictures more closely. She looked quizzically at Laurence. "Are you making fun of my child? You really think so?"

"I sure do. You need to discuss this with her teachers. They can help her develop her skills. It would be a shame for her to waste such a gift."

Although Jenny seemed pleased by his comments and interest, she looked away, clearly embarrassed. "Yes. Sure. I will speak to her teachers. I'll show them these pictures," she said in a low voice.

Laurence regretted the patronizing way he had spoken to her. "Hey, I'm not trying to tell you how to bring up Chloe. I just want her to have her due. Kids like her should be made to feel special."

"I always make my daughter feel special," she said defensively. "By the way, today is Chloe's last day here. She won't have to be a concern of yours any more." She took the drawings and stalked out of his office with her head held high.

Returning to the reception room, Jenny found her daughter slumped and sulking on the sofa. Her coloring book and crayons had been tossed aside.

Chloe gave her mother a sad look. "Mommy, what time are we going home? I want to call Aunt Nina and Uncle Addison."

Jenny knew that Chloe's desire to talk with her godparents was a sure sign she was unhappy about the punishment her mother had promised her. The punishment for bad behavior was always no television and no dessert for the evening.

"We can't call them tonight. Aunt Nina told me they would be busy attending evening lectures all the week. We're going to have to call them on the weekend," she told the child.

Chloe swung her legs back and forth, making an annoying thumping noise against the sofa with her feet. "Mr. Strong doesn't like me. He gives me mean looks."

Jenny took a seat at her computer and attempted to complete a letter that was due for the day. "Mr. Strong is a busy man with a lot on his mind. I'm sure he likes you. It's just that he isn't used to being around children. That's all, sweetheart. And wouldn't you be upset with him if he came to our house and went in your bedroom and went through your favorite things the way you did with his stuff today?"

Chloe gave her mother a look that showed she understood. "He would make me mad. Is he going to do that to get even with me?"

Jenny grinned at her daughter. "No, baby, he's not. But I'm glad you understand how he feels. Whenever you come here with me, you must not go in his office and bother his things. Okay?"

"Yes, Mommy, I promise," Chloe said.

Laurence appeared at his door. "Chloe, would you come here, please?" he asked in a serious voice.

Chloe's eyes widened and she gave her mother a helpless look.

Jenny swung her gaze to Laurence to check out his emotions. Her mind was set at ease when he winked and smiled at her.

"Chloe, go on and see what Mr. Strong wants," Jenny urged.

Chloe slid off the sofa and shuffled into the man's office as though she were going to her doom.

Jenny got up from her work and went to the half-opened door to observe what would happen.

Laurence handed Chloe one of his oversized sketch pads. "I want you to draw in this and not on my plans. And don't throw away any of the pictures you do. When the book is filled, I want you to show them to me and tell me all about what you have drawn and why. After you've filled up this sketch pad, I will give you another one, along with a box of crayons or colored pencils." He smiled at the child, thinking how much she looked like her lovely mother. "Do we have a deal?"

Chloe held the pad to her solid body as though she had been given something priceless.

Her eyes sparkled with excitement. "Yes, Mr. Strong," she answered, whirling away from him and back to her mother.

Jenny stared at Laurence with admiration. She was touched by the motivation to draw he had given Chloe. "Sweetheart, tell Mr. Strong thank you."

"Thank you," Chloe enthused and dashed past her mother into the reception room.

Laurence's eyes met Jenny's.

The twinkle in Laurence's eyes and the dazzle in his smile was as sweet as a kiss would have been. Jenny felt all aglow from the spark. "That was really kind of you."

Laurence shrugged. "It's no big deal. I know she is really a good kid." He spoke in a gentle tone.

"I'm just about done for the day," she said, feeling cheered by the compliment about Chloe. "Chloe and I will be leaving in a bit." She turned to leave.

"Jenny," he called, his voice sounding urgent. Jenny paused and stared at him. She was caught off guard by the vibrancy of his tone.

He looked like he wanted to say something important. But he shook his head, hesitated. "Have you prepared all the information we need for my presentation at the architecture convention?" he said at last.

She nodded confidently. "I'm almost done. I have a few more things to do on Monday. Then everything will be ready for you to check over."

"Good. Very good."

She smiled shyly and left his office.

Laurence walked to his window and looked out onto the busy downtown streets, thinking of how he had gotten to know Jenny since she had come to work for him. He couldn't believe how awkward Jenny had made him feel just now. Normally, he had a smooth delivery that could charm the panties off any woman he wanted. But the emotion he felt blossoming for Jenny was more than a sexual thing. He had wanted to ask her out to dinner, but had thought better of it. He knew that she would probably come up with some excuse. He had been lacking in charm around her in the office. Still, he wished that he could have an opportunity to be alone with Jenny so they could talk personally, intimately. At last he had met a woman that he wanted to be a friend as well as a lover and a companion. But she came with a kid. He thought he had been ready to deal with a child. Yet he hadn't been as patient as he thought he should have been with Chloe. The stress of his two offices in two different states left him edgy and overwhelmed at times. Though he had vowed to himself to go easy on Jenny, he hadn't followed through on this issue. He had taken out his frustrations on her. He had been short-tempered and impatient. He reasoned that he had acted this way because he had hoped to rid himself of his interest in her. He knew that if things got cozy between himself and Jenny, he was going to have to share her with Chloe. From what he had observed of Jenny, she was a good and devoted mother. He figured that after all she had been through with her failed marriage, she had lost respect and serious interest in the male species. She probably feared getting hurt again.

Laurence heard the office door to the reception area close, and the sound of a key being turned. He went to look in Jenny's office and saw that her desk had been straightened for the day. Normally, he welcomed the solitude of his office. Now, with Jenny and Chloe gone, he suddenly found that he was filled with loneliness. He walked to the window behind Jenny's desk. Glancing out the window, he caught a glimpse of Jenny and Chloe, walking hand in hand toward the parking lot to her secondhand car. Chloe carried the sketch pad as though she were a little businesswoman. He admired the sight of them until they were out of sight. He intended to show Jenny, on their trip to Virginia Beach, that he could be pleasant and worth getting to know.

***

Though Jenny had made it clear to Chloe that she would only be gone for two days, she could see that her daughter wasn't happy to be separated from her. She had given Chloe the phone number of the hotel where she and Mr. Strong would be staying, and had encouraged her to call in the evening.

Laurence had arrived at seven-thirty that morning. The heat and humidity of the day could already be felt. Jenny had packed a medium-sized suitcase which was fully packed and heavy. He placed her bag in the trunk of his car beside his. He noticed that Chloe watched his actions quietly. The usually energetic child was quiet and sad looking. He attempted to talk to her, but she showed no interest for his conversation concerning her plans while her mother was away. Chloe's behavior made him feel a bit self-conscious about taking her mother off to work with him.

Jenny was wearing a pink pullover shirt and a short denim skirt and sandals for their road trip. She came and stood beside her daughter and draped her arm around her child's shoulder. "I'll be back before you know it," she told Chloe, cupping her chin and tilting her face toward her. "And I will be back, sweetheart," she assured her, knowing the little girl hadn't forgotten the time her mother had deserted her.

Laurence watched Jenny and Chloe with interest. The bond between them was touching.

He thought of his old man and how they hadn't connected, and felt a tinge of envy. He cleared his throat to get Jenny's attention. "We've got to get on the road," he reminded her in a good-natured tone, getting into the car to wait for her to finish her good-byes.

"Sure. I'm ready," she said. She stooped to hug Chloe and give her a good-bye kiss. "I'll call you as soon as I arrive and get settled," she promised her. She released her daughter and got into Laurence's car.

Jenny stared at her forlorn-looking daughter, who stood between the Hollands, holding their hands.

"Don't worry, honey. Chloe will be fine with us," Mrs. Holland told an anxious Jenny. "We'll keep her busy, so she won't miss you so much."

"Thanks again," Jenny called to the Hollands.

Laurence grew slightly impatient and started the car to end the lengthy scene. If he hadn't given this signal, he feared they might be wasting even more travel time than they already had.

As the car moved down the street, Jenny leaned out the window to wave at her daughter until Laurence turned the corner. Jenny flopped morosely in her seat and fastened her seat belt. She dug in her purse for tissues to wipe her eyes, which were filled with tears.

Laurence stared at her with a baffled expression. "My goodness, you're only going on a short trip. She's old enough to understand that."

Jenny sniffled and donned her wire-framed sunglasses against the bright June sun. "Chloe is thinking that she might not see me again."

"Kids. I suppose they allow their imaginations to run away with them, huh?" He made a turn that led to an entrance to the interstate.

Jenny sighed. "They can. But Chloe has a reason to be scared. You see, I did desert her for a short while. It's one of those things that I regret," she said woefully. "I haven't always been a good mother." She laughed nervously. Then she rested her head against the headrest and turned away as though she felt she had already said too much.

Laurence was stunned by her confession. He couldn't imagine Jenny being so thoughtless to Chloe. Then he considered how at times he had caught her staring into space and how her brown eyes often looked weary and sad, as though her heart were breaking.

***

For the first two hours of the trip, Jenny napped. She didn't want to talk more than she had to. Had they been in the office, they could have spoken about work that needed to be done. Whenever they had a conversation about anything besides business, she worried that she wasn't speaking correct English. Laurence was well educated and well read. He had a wonderful voice.

When Jenny was uncomfortable, she was embarrassed by the way she mumbled, not sure of how to express herself professionally. On the other hand, Laurence spoke clearly and with a confidence that was at times thrilling as well as intimidating.

After she awoke, Jenny stole glimpses of Laurence's chest and arms. He wore a red pullover short-sleeved shirt. He had great biceps, a broad chest, trim waist and flat stomach. She took notice of his full lips, Which caused her to wonder how they felt engaged in kissing. His heavenly tawny eyes burned with intensity, with his constant ambition to succeed and to be the best. Occasionally, she had walked in on him at the office and caught him staring into space with a faraway, pensive look that made him appear vulnerable. She had often wondered what put that look there. She had noticed that the expression appeared whenever his father's caregiver, Jeremy, called. Otherwise, Laurence acted as though he needed no one and that he could take on the world all on his own.

"We should be in Virginia Beach soon," Laurence announced, breaking her reverie.

Jenny glanced at her watch. "That'll give us more than enough time to go to our rooms to relax, change and freshen up before that three o'clock session you want to attend."

"We can stop and get a bite to eat before we arrive. I don't know about you, but I'm famished. I packed at the last minute and didn't take time for breakfast," he said.

"Sounds good to me. I could use something to eat myself," Jenny agreed, thinking about the cereal she had watched her child eat that morning, without having any appetite herself. She had been too uptight about the trip and proving to Laurence that she could handle the responsibility he had given her.

Laurence stopped at a waffle and steak house just off the interstate.

"How has your father been feeling? I've been thinking about him, though I haven't had a chance to visit him," Jenny said, taking a sip of her second cup of coffee. She had met the man once when she had taken a prescription to Marvin Strong's house as a favor to Jeremy. Marvin Strong had been friendly toward her. He had inquired about her family background and her daughter. He had explained that he knew just about everyone in Harper Falls. Before she had left, Mr. Strong had told her to return and to bring her little girl the next time. He had teased her and said that he and Jeremy welcomed whatever feminine company they could get. Jenny had found the invalid man delightful. And she had intended to visit again when her schedule allowed.

Laurence's eyes shifted uneasily. "He's doing fair. He's just a bit stubborn when it comes to his therapy and staying on his diet." He looked at Jenny and gave her a warm smile. "You made quite an impression on him when you ran that errand. He is anxious to meet your little girl."

"Chloe and I are going to have to make a point of getting by there, real soon."

"He'll like that," Laurence said. "Whenever I visit him, he quizzes me about you."

Jenny heard a tinge of envy in his voice, and wondered what was the relationship between father and son.

"I suppose your moving back to Harper Falls has meant a lot to him," Jenny said.

"I don't know about that. There isn't too much I can do to impress my old man," he said in a reluctant manner.

"I can't believe that. You're the kind of son any man should be proud to have. You and he only have each other, don't you? That's a special bond, you know." Her brow wrinkled sadly. "I know about that. I only have Chloe and she means the world to me. She keeps me pressing on, even when I feel I can't face another day. It's tough being on my own with her. I imagine you've been the same kind of inspiration for your father, in the rough days he's had to endure since his accident."

Laurence smiled tightly and sipped at his coffee. "Yeah, sure," he said dryly.

Their relationship couldn't be good, Jenny thought, but Laurence was the kind of man with too much pride to show his feelings.

After an uncomfortable silence, Laurence gave Jenny a strange look of curiosity. "You have no other family in the area, huh?"

She smiled timidly, considering how much of her past she wanted to divulge to Laurence.

She decided to confide in him. "The closest person to family I have is Nina Wagner. She's like a sister to me." She took a deep breath, searching his eyes for his thoughts . "She and I shared the same foster home for a few years. I was a scared little girl and she was older. She took me under her wing and protected me and loved me more than anyone I had ever known. Then she and I were separated. The foster mother we had didn't like Nina and had her sent away. It broke my heart to have her snatched out of my life. After that, I was alone and lonely. In my teen years, I fell into bad company with awful men. I had Chloe by a boy whom I had planned to marry until he was killed in some kind of gang mess. Depressed and afraid of being on my own, I married Chloe's father's best friend. It turned out to be one of the worst mistakes in my life. Then fate brought Nina back into my life. I was so proud to discover that she had gone to college and had become a doctor. Unlike many of us stranded in foster care, Nina had made it. She reached out to me when I needed her, and we've remained close ever since." She sighed and waited for his response to the grim past she had shared with him.

Laurence's throat constricted from what he had heard of Jenny's life; his heart wrung with pity. He cleared his throat and spoke softly. "What...what a tough road you've had. Plenty of people don't make it under the kind of circumstances you had to endure. You're quite a lady. I'm proud to know someone like you with such courage."

His admiration sent her spirits soaring. She appreciated him empathizing with her instead of pitying her.

He settled a kind smile on her. "So that's how you and Nina Wagner are connected." Staring at Jenny with interest, he found it difficult to mask the sympathy he felt. He had been aware of her abusive marriage, but to learn that she had been an orphan as well softened his heart for her even more. Now he understood why she sometimes acted like a shrinking violet. "I can't believe that a woman as classy as Nina was in foster care. She doesn't fit the stereotype at all. I always thought she was part of that upper middle class social group that Addison had grown up in."

"Nina was always a good student. That was her ticket out. I, on the other hand, wasn't as bright. I bought the idea that I needed a man to rescue me. I got involved with all the wrong kinds of guys, looking for love in anyone who showed me a crumb of kindness," she admitted. "I only complicated my life by thinking a man could save me. But it was the only way I could see to set myself free from the system that was full of horrible memories."

Noticing the way her lovely mouth quivered and seeing her eyes pool with tears, Laurence wanted to touch her hand. But he didn't. He didn't want her to feel as though he were pitying her. He signaled the waitress for their check.

Jenny sighed and blinked her eyes, forcing a smile. "You know, I often admire that picture of you and your family on your desk. I understand your brother died young. What happened to him?" Since she had opened up to him, she saw no harm in questioning him about his personal life.

He grunted, looked away from her, and signaled the waitress once more.

She rushed over and handed Laurence their check. He was grateful for her presence. He didn't yet want to delve into the details of his own life, with Jenny. "He died in a car wreck," he answered curtly. He pulled out his wallet and concentrated on the amount of the bill.

"I see," Jenny said, catching the hint that he didn't want to share the situation with her. She hadn't missed the fact that his eyes had clouded at the mention of the circumstances of his brother's death.

Laurence stood. "Let's go. I want to get to the hotel, so that you'll have plenty of time to set up the conference room. I have some people who will be waiting on me as well."

Jenny sighed. Just for a moment, she had had the enjoyment of their conversation and their time alone. It had made her feel as though she were a date, instead of a secretary on a business trip. But the warmth on Laurence's face had faded, and once more she was reminded that she was only his employee.

Chapter 6

It wasn't until Jenny and Laurence reached the hotel in Virginia Beach and gone to their separate rooms that Jenny discovered that she had marked the wrong boxes to be loaded for the trip. Checking each box, which was supposed to contain the carefully prepared folders and the videos for Laurence's lecture, Jenny nearly fainted with panic to see that all that they had were office supplies. There was no doubt in her mind; she would lose her job. Laurence had two sessions to speak at the next day. He needed those videos; he needed the folders with the information she had worked so hard on, creating graphics and designs to enhance his presentation. She fled to his room to reveal her mistake.

"You did what?" Laurence exclaimed, scowling at a humbled Jenny, who stood at the door of his room.

Her eyes drooped with shame. "I'm sorry. Really sorry," she said in a low, tormented voice. "I guess I was distracted. I had brought Chloe with me that evening I was packing the materials. The Hollands couldn't keep her. They had appointments with their doctor," she explained. "While I was separating the material and marking the boxes, she slipped into your office. I stopped to get her out because I didn't want her to make a mess like she had done before and..."

Laurence's tawny eyes grew blank. He whirled away from her and stormed over to the telephone. "Come inside," he ordered in a gruff tone, then cursed softly. "I can't have a decent seminar without those things." He rubbed the back of his neck and sighed deeply with frustration, then picked up the phone.

Seeing his disappointment, Jenny reluctantly slipped inside his room and shut the door. She stood with her arms hugging her body as though something awful was about to happen. She knew all too well about the man's temper. Since she had worked for Laurence, she had seen how enraged he could get when it came to his work or anything that represented him. Watching him stand in the middle of the floor looking both angry and befuddled, she wondered morosely if they had any openings at Wal-Mart. She was certain that he was about to fire her and give her traveling money to return to Harper Falls.

Suddenly, a flicker of hope slashed Laurence's face as he talked on the phone. "Roscoe, man, am I glad to catch you home," Laurence said. His face revealed his relief. "I need to ask a big favor." He turned away from Jenny and spoke confidently to the man whom Jenny disliked. Roscoe Baker, the prosecuting attorney.

Jenny didn't know whether to stay or leave. She didn't want Laurence to feel as though she were eavesdropping. She really wanted to be out of his presence and the humiliation she experienced because of her stupidity.

Laurence slammed the phone down and turned on his heels to face Jenny. He slapped his hands together and came toward her.

Watching his hands, Jenny jumped and stepped back. Earl had had a movement like that. One minute she would think everything was cool and the next moment he would deliver a blow so hard that she would land on the floor on her behind.

But Laurence gave her a relieved smile. "Roscoe is going to Fed Ex the material to us. We should get it in time for that first session tomorrow."

Jenny's body relaxed from the news. "Mr. Baker has the key to your office?"

"Of course not. He's going to get the janitor to let him into the office to get the stuff. I'm going to owe that rascal big time," he said with affection. "He told me he'll be here for the weekend, too. He's visiting friends." The lines of worry had faded.

Jenny wasn't looking forward to running into Roscoe Baker. However, she was glad that he would be able to clear up the awful blunder she had made. "Will the package be delivered to your room or mine?" she asked, making her way to the door.

Laurence followed her. "It will come to the front desk of the hotel before noon. Can I count on you to get it and arrange things in the conference room we've been assigned?"

"I'll take care of everything."

Laurence stared at her skeptically. Then he glanced at his watch. "I have to get changed. I have some networking to do." He opened the door for her.

Jenny hurried into the hallway. "I'm glad that's taken care of."

"So am I," he said. "See you at the afternoon session," he said, closing the door.

Jenny decided not to let her thoughts linger on how abrupt he had been. She knew he had a lot on his mind. She was grateful that he hadn't gotten angry enough to fire her. She hustled off to change her clothes and to prepare for the session that did-n't require anything but her presence to show her support for Laurence.

***

Jenny attended the first session the day they arrived at the hotel. Laurence hardly needed her presence. He was welcomed and surrounded by eager members of the convention who wanted to

meet and chat with him. Jenny made it her business to locate the agenda that would be followed
during the their two-day stay to give to Laurence
later. Laurence caught up with her after that initial
session and told her that he had made plans with
some of the attendees to go out for the evening. He
suggested that she relax for the rest of the evening.
Before he hurried off to be with his peers, he
reminded her to keep checking on the package they
were expecting from Roscoe.

Jenny had dinner alone in a nearby restaurant
and returned to her room. She called the Hollands
and chatted with Chloe, who answered the phone
on the first ring. Jenny imagined that her child had
probably sat near the phone anxiously awaiting her
call to make sure that she kept her promise. Worn
out from the excitement of the day, Jenny went to
bed early with a new romance novel she had
brought to keep her company.

The next morning she was awakened by a
phone call from Laurence. He informed her of the
free Continental breakfast that was available for
the guests. He mentioned that he wouldn't be
there. He had stayed out late the night before and
planned to sleep in until it was time for his sessions. Once more he reminded Jenny not to forget
the front desk for the package.

After Jenny had eaten breakfast, she checked
the front desk; sure enough, the package had

arrived for them. She had it taken to the conference room where Laurence was scheduled to speak.

Once Laurence had completed his last presentation for the day, Jenny experienced a deep sense of pride and satisfaction. She had had nightmares of ruining everything for Laurence by not compiling the detailed handouts and the copies of his sketches on time. But she had pulled it all together in spite of the mix-up with the boxes. Her ego had been boosted by her achievement.

After Laurence had chatted with the last members of his seminar, he strolled toward Jenny wearing a cheerful expression. "Great job," he said, lavishing her with a special smile.

"Everyone thinks you're the greatest. They told me I'd better treat you right or else they would try to lure you away."

Jenny's eyes glinted with pleasure. "Hmm...I doubt if they could persuade me to leave Harper Falls. But it's nice to know that my work is appreciated." For the first time in weeks, she was able to look him straight in the eye. She liked the glow of satisfaction on his face. Today's effort had proven that they worked well as a team.

Today Jenny had seen Laurence turn up the charm for the participants in his group. Watching him, her feminine sensibilities had become electrified. He looked dapper in his designer suit, and the light fragrance of his cologne made her feel heady.

Jenny couldn't take being near Laurence for long, feeling the way she did. She eased away from him, trying to keep her hands busy by clearing away the left-behind materials, keeping her feet moving. Otherwise, she felt she might give away the fact that she had fallen under his spell.

Laurence was equally intrigued by Jenny. She had come dressed more professionally than he had ever seen. She wore a tailored suit and blouse. He loved watching the way her body swayed with the help of her high-heeled pumps. "Do you need any help clearing away the videos and other materials? I can't help you. I have some people to meet with. But I can see to it that someone here in the hotel gives you a hand."

She smiled. "I'm fine. I got one of the hotel guys to bring a cart for me to transport all this back to my room until the final session tomorrow."

Laurence noticed for the first time that the joy of Jenny's smile placed a twinkle in her eyes. That look inspired a feeling of excitement that he hadn't experienced in years. He admired the simple yet tasteful gray of the suit that she had worn. He also liked the way the red blouse she wore accented her lovely café au lait coloring. Her wavy hair was shiny and fluffy; it had that tousled look that caused him to wonder if that was the way she looked after a night of passionate lovemaking. During his presentation he had caught several of the men checking out Jenny's marvelous form. He wouldn't be a bit surprised if one or two of them had approached her for a date as a way of keeping in touch with her. The thought made him jealous. But what right did he have to keep her from dating anyone?

Curious to see if anyone had hit on her for a date, Laurence asked, "What are you doing this evening?"

She stared up at him. "Relaxing and enjoying my lovely hotel room like I did last night. I'm going to get some dinner, then return to my room to call my daughter. The rest of the evening will be spent reading the romance novel I brought along to entertain myself." While she talked, she stacked the remaining materials in neat piles.

Laurence gave her an amused look. "Romance novel? You read that junk?"

Jenny nodded, giving him a languid smile. "I'm a sucker for stories with those happily-ever-after endings," she admitted. "Whenever I read one, I get a chance to fall in love with a tall, dark and handsome man. I think of it as safe sex." She chuckled. "No heartaches, no complicated relationships to send me off the deep end. Once I complete a book, I can move on to the next one and fall in love all over again and share someone else's romance and world."

Laurence grunted amiably. "Why live other people's fantasies when a young woman like yourself could be experiencing a romance of your own?"

"Uh-uh. I've had my taste of romance and it brought me nothing but heartache and trouble. It made a complete fool of me. No more," she declared.

He knew the feeling. He felt the same way about romance. He had had his share of women, and he had grown tired of the games and complications in relationships. He had been so busy building his career and businesses that he had denied himself the pleasure of any serious relationship. "I can sympathize with your feelings. But I'm sure there's someone, somewhere, who can give you everything that you deserve. You could even find someone to make you feel as though you're living your own romance novel." Laurence felt as though he were talking too much. If he wasn't careful, he might let her see that he wished to have a chance with her himself. He glanced at his watch. "Enough of my lecturing. I have to get out of here. Listen, I should be done by ten o'clock tonight. How about me coming to get you and take you out for a walk on the beach? Or perhaps we could go to one of the lounges and listen to some music and have a drink." He felt silly for the roundabout way he was asking for a date. "I want you to remember the city for more than just the hard work you've put into making me look good."

His self-conscious invitation stunned her. Was he actually asking her for a date? "Uh...sure, I'd like that."

"See you later," he enthused, striding out of the conference room.

At his exit, Jenny took a seat in the nearest chair, kicked off her new pumps and wriggled her toes. Laurence Strong had asked her out, she mused. Was she wrong to have accepted the invitation from her boss? She tried to convince herself that she shouldn't make anything out of the evening. He was only attempting to do the gentlemanly thing and show her around. However, Jenny had caught the glimmer in his eyes and heard the velvet-smooth timbre in his voice.

Jenny thought of the length of time she hadn't slept with a man. It had been nearly three years. A long time to be celibate for a woman who had loved sex—especially when she had believed she was in love. She missed sex. Passion. Lately she had found herself wondering what kind of lover Laurence could be. She had eyed him at the office. She liked watching the slow, smooth manner of his walk. Whenever she could steal glances of him hunched over his drafting table and deep in thought as he etched out his creative designs, she found him simply endearing. And today, during the seminar he had held, she had taken time to see a side of him that was utterly fabulous. She could clearly see why he had the number of clients he had. Not only was he a creative and innovative genius, but he was an eloquent speaker who had been quite capable of holding everyone's rapt attention. While he discussed his latest structures and the latest architectural trends, Jenny had heard in his voice the passion he had for his work, and had seen it on his face as well. She wondered if people like him, who had such passion for their work, could be as fervent for their woman in bed. With that thought, she closed her eyes and rested her head on the back of the chair. She created images of Laurence and herself, lying on a deserted beach in the moonlight....

Laurence wore tight trunks that emphasized his manhood. She wore a skimpy two-piece bathing suit that revealed every inch of her shapely body. They had swum in the ocean and returned to the shore to roll and tumble in each other's arms on the sand. The moon had a hypnotic effect on them. They couldn't keep their hands off each other. No words were spoken. They didn't need words to say what they both felt on such a glorious night. Passion, hot and electrifying. Laurence smothered Jenny with his magnificent form, delivering heated kisses and delightful nibbles to her neck and lips. She embraced his broad shoulders and parted her lips to receive his probing tongue. Her blood sizzled

and the center of her body ached. She moaned from
the sweetness of his kisses. Soon his kisses were
accompanied by searching caresses that wandered
from the curve of her waist, her hips, to the inside
of her thighs. Jenny's mind grew cloudy with her
arousal and Laurence's ardent desire. He undid the
top of her suit to free her breasts; he fell upon
them, nuzzling them with his face. He took each
swollen tip between his lips and flicked his tongue
over and around it, causing her to become even
more drugged with lust. She slipped her hands into
the back of his trunks and scooted them down over
his hips, freeing his manly steel. He assisted her by
removing them completely. Then he tugged away
the bottom of her suit. They clung to each other,
relishing the feel of their heated flesh in lustful tan-
dem. Their excitement mounted with each kiss,
each tender touch here and there. His rigid manhood throbbed near her love cove, tantalizing her.
She spread her legs, inviting him inside. Laurence
positioned himself between her thighs and penetrated her with a groan of delight...

"Ms. Martin. Yo! Ms. Martin!"

Startled by the sound of the voice, Jenny bolted upright in her seat. Breathing hard as though
she had really made love, she blinked at the col-
lege-age hotel employee who had come to assist
her.

The young man seemed to be amused by the way she had reacted at being caught snoozing. "I didn't mean to scare you, ma'am. I've got the cart in the hall," he informed her. "Is this what you want loaded and taken to your room?" He nodded toward the clutter on the table.

She stood and slipped on her shoes again. "Yeah. Please get those videos and boxes over in the corner first," she instructed.

While the guy worked, she watched him, running her hand through her hair to clear her mind of her dream. She was amazed by the way her body still tingled from the erotic dream that had seemed so real. Oh boy, she thought, scooping up supplies to help the guy, she was going to have to find a way to kill the kind of fantasy she had had. She didn't want to make a fool of herself on this business trip. She thought of the date she had with Laurence later. Anxiety coursed through her. She had missed sensual pleasure and the feel of a man's body to comfort her. Though she had tried to ignore her desires, she had missed that part of being a woman terribly. She hoped that being alone with a fine looking brother like Laurence on a summer's night wouldn't cause her to do anything that she might come to regret later.

***

Jenny had been lost in her reading of her new romance novel, *Love Under the Stars*, when Laurence called to say he was on his way to meet her.

She tossed aside her novel and hurried into her floral-patterned sundress. She pushed up her hair on both sides, using glittering bobby pins to accent her hair. The hairdo showed off her gold hoop earrings. Hearing a rap on the door, Jenny studied herself in the mirror one final time before opening it for her boss.

The moment she came face to face with him, she was hit with the memory of her erotic fantasy that afternoon. The sight of him left her nearly breathless. Laurence had changed from his suit into khaki slacks and a pullover black t-shirt, which clung to his well-built physique. Jenny decided that he looked as though he had stepped right off the pages of the romance novel she had been reading.

"You look lovely, Ms. Martin." Laurence's eyes glowed with delight. "Let's go."

Jenny grinned as though she were a schoolgirl as she left her room with the handsomest man in the city. Walking down the hall toward the elevator with Laurence at her side, Jenny had a feeling that something would happen that would change her ordinary life. Out of the corners of her eyes, she could feel Laurence scrutinizing her hair and her shoulders. A hot flash shot through her. Was she about to embark on an adventure like the beautiful, sophisticated heroine in her novel?

Sitting in the hotel lounge in a cozy corner with Laurence, Jenny felt as if all the responsibilities and worries from the last few years had fallen away from her. She and Laurence had a round of drinks. The female singer sang mellow romantic tunes that made Jenny wish she could have one more chance to know what it was like to have a loving relationship. But she considered that wishful thinking. She believed she had wasted her wonderful gift of love on the losers who had entered and nearly ruined her life.

In the dimly lit lounge, Jenny became captive to the personable side of Laurence. His slow, easy smiles accompanied by lingering looks whenever she spoke made her feel vivacious.

Laurence rested his hand on the table near hers. "You're telling me you haven't dated since you and your old man split?" he asked. Laurence admired Jenny's flawless complexion and her smooth shoulders. His fingers ached to touch her exposed flesh.

"No men. I've been too busy taking care of myself and my daughter. I may have failed in marriage, but I'm determined to be a good mother. I want to set a good example for my Chloe," she said with conviction. "I intend to get to college somehow and to have a decent career. Obtaining these things is more important than having a man."

Though he was skeptical of what she had said, Laurence gave her an admiring look. "College? That's pretty ambitious. How in the world will you swing that with a kid and a job?"

"I'll manage. Women do it all the time. In fact, there are a couple of women in my support group who have done it and others who are working toward goals like mine."

Laurence folded his arms and leaned forward on the table. "I don't mean to pry. But what kind of support group is this?"

Jenny ran her fingers through the back of her hair to flick it off her neck. Ever since she had been with Laurence this evening, her body had felt fevered. She wished she hadn't brought up her support group. She was telling this man too much of her private life.

Jenny considered brushing off his comment. Instead, she decided to be straightforward with him. "It's a group of women who...who have been abused by their spouses or boyfriends the way I was," she explained. "I don't know what I would have done without it. After I knew deep in my heart that I had no desire to salvage my marriage or to be associated with my husband, I nearly fell apart emotionally. I felt as though I was being suffocated by the ugliness of the reality I had refused to deal with before." She paused to take a sip of her wine and to calm her nerves. Her brow furrowed and her eyes darkened as the vivid memories of the pain and fear returned. "Oh, there was a major mess that brought me to my senses. I had the respected Wagners, pillars of the community, entangled in it, too. It was enough for them to cut their ties with me for good. But they didn't. Thank goodness. And I love them for all they've ever done for me, and especially Chloe."

Seeing the sadness on her face, Laurence reached over and touched Jenny's hand to encourage her to continue to speak. It wasn't that he was nosey. He was genuinely concerned over the tragic events of her life. "What was the turning point? What happened?"

His sincere interest touched her wounded heart. She continued, "My husband went on a drug binge with his friends. He had left me and my daughter alone with no money or food. I was sick with a virus and depressed over the trouble and danger I'd placed myself in. We were dead broke. I happened to overhear my husband talking with his friends about selling my child to a rich couple for thousands of dollars. He intended on using the sale of my baby to keep himself supplied with all the drugs he ever needed. Not only was he going to sell her, but his plans were to show up every now and then to harass the people, to milk them for more money or threaten to take my child back from them."

Scowling, Laurence shook his head. "What a piece of...What kind of man is diabolic enough to sell a child?"

Jenny took hold of Laurence's hand and squeezed it as though she was drawing strength to go on. "A man who has turned into a monster by his drug addiction."

Frowning with concern, he took hold of Jenny's other hand. His heart ached for all the horrid events she'd revealed so far.

Jenny cleared her throat of the emotion and the shame she felt; she had been tied up in that awful situation for too long. "Hearing what Earl's plans were, concerning Chloe, I had to leave him. I borrowed money from a kind, elderly woman to get out of town, and return to Harper Falls and to Nina's. Soon after Chloe and I returned, Earl showed up to demand that I come back with him. When he couldn't talk me into leaving, he grabbed Chloe and tried to make off with her. He held Nina and me off with a gun. Thankfully, Addison showed up in time. He managed to rescue Chloe. Earl tried to shoot Addison. The police arrived and the next thing I knew we were all on the late news broadcast and in the newspaper." She removed her hands from his and covered her face. She wept softly. She hadn't spoken of the day often. But whenever she dredged it up, it had the same disturbing effect on her. The pain and humiliation of the mess was still stark and scary. She couldn't help but wonder what would have happened if Earl had gotten away with Chloe.

Laurence scooted his chair closer to Jenny. He placed his arm around her shoulder and rested his face next to hers as though it was something he was used to doing. Even though he didn't know her on such a personal level, he couldn't resist touching her to show that he sympathized with her pain.

Jenny lowered her hands and made an effort to smile through her tears. She used a cocktail napkin to wipe her eyes. "Just think, that happened nearly three years ago and I'm still making a fool of myself over it." She looked into Laurence's eyes and saw compassion that was like a balm.

He held her gaze. He brushed the side of her face with the tip of his finger. "You have nothing to be ashamed of. You're to be admired for rising above something like that."

Jenny's heart swelled with gratitude for the look of tenderness she saw on his face.

Laurence reached for his wallet and flung some money on the table. "Let's get out of here. Go for a walk. The night air is what we need," he said in a silky voice. He stood to help her with her chair. He placed his hand at the base of her back and escort-

ed her out of the place, smiling affectionately at
her.

Chapter 7

Walking along the shore, Jenny was glad that the summer night was cooler and breezier than it had been earlier in the day. It was wonderful strolling with Laurence under the watchful eyes of the moon and the stars.

Laurence slipped his hand into Jenny's. "I have some good memories of this city. My parents used to bring us here to vacation. Gary...Gary, my brother, and I loved the ocean and loved to swim. We were wild kids and used to drive my mother insane with our darling antics in the water. You see, my brother and I dreamed of being the first blacks to win gold medals for swimming in the Olympics." He grew quiet; he looked pensively out to the ocean and stared as though he could see images of himself and his brother when they were kids, frolicking in the water and on the beach. He squeezed her hand, consumed by sadness of the way things had been.

Jenny tried to remain cool from the hand-holding deal with Laurence. She could sense that his memories of his lost sibling required someone's comfort.

"Tell me what happened to him," Jenny said, hoping that Laurence would share the incident with her.

"Hmm...I'll tell you some other time. Right now, let's just enjoy the sounds and the smell of the ocean and the beauty of the sky." He proceeded to lead her down a path that led to big boulders located on the shore, where they could sit.

"Oh, my goodness, I imagine it's incredible here during the day," she said, perching herself next to him on one of the rocks. She looped her arm with his. "Let me hold on to you. I don't want to fall into the ocean. I can't swim a lick," she said. She chuckled softly.

Laurence liked her being near him. He slipped an arm around her waist, gripping it gently. "Relax. You'll be fine. I won't let you go tumbling into the water." He laughed.

Once he was sure that Jenny was settled, he stared at the lovely silhouette of her face as she looked out toward the ocean.

Isolated in this spot, Jenny felt as though she and Laurence were the only two people in the world. Inspired by the soothing sound of the water and the backdrop of the star-filled sky, she yearned to be crushed in his embrace. She wanted to feel as though she were one of those romance novel's heroines. With his arm around her waist, hooking her protectively from her fear of falling, she experience feelings of desire she knew she had no business feeling for her boss.

Laurence turned toward her. He spoke close to her ear to be heard above the roar of the ocean. "I wish I could bottle the tranquility and beauty of the night. It would be great to take it back to Harper Falls and unleash it in times of stress and trouble."

The warmth of his breath caused a delicious tickling sensation in the pit of her stomach.

He kept his face close to hers and stared out at the majestic ocean. Growing self-conscious from his piercing looks, Jenny reached up and smoothed the side of her hair. When she did this, she snagged her fancy bobby pin, tugging it out. That side of her long hair fell free. She attempted to pin up her hair again, but Laurence caught her hand.

"Don't. Let if fall free," he urged in a whisper. He pulled the bobby pin from the other side as well. "There. That's much better." He watched her hair as it was tossed by the wind from one side to the other. He ran his fingers through her lustrous tangled tresses, holding one side in place in order to place a tender kiss upon her lips.

With that kiss, her consciousness seemed to ebb and then flame more distinctly than ever.

She allowed him to hold her to him and to share several sweet kisses. His lips on hers revitalized every fiber within her. She embraced his shoulders. Pressed together as best they could in their awkward sitting position on the boulder, Jenny felt his heart beating as hard as hers. She was thrilled that her fantasy had become a reality. The moment was magic and full of sweet tenderness.

Breaking their embrace to catch their breaths, the two sat snuggled together, staring at the wonders of the night. Jenny realized that the boundary she had crossed could have serious consequences. What kind of working relationship could they have, now that they had given in to their physical attraction to one another?

"Shouldn't we head back to the hotel?" Jenny suggested even though she wanted to stay.

She wanted to hear him say that he didn't want to leave either.

He caressed the side of her arm with his palm. "There's no reason to hurry back. Let's stay a while longer."

Relishing his touch and the chemistry between them, she murmured, "Laurence, I have a bad feeling about this. This isn't right for us...me."

He pressed a kiss upon her cheek. "You're wrong. This is right. We're two people who are attracted to one another. There's nothing wrong with that. I have a feeling that neither one of us will ever forget this feeling or this night."

She leaned away from him just a bit to speak. "I work for you. Until the last couple of weeks, we have barely been able to work together. Now we're here on the beach at night and falling into each other's arms. We're asking for trouble."

Carefully rising to his feet on the boulder, he held out a hand to Jenny. "I don't see it that way. But since you're uncomfortable, let's go." He pulled her to her feet to lead the way back down to the shore. Once he leapt to the sand, he reached up and fitted his hands around her trim waist; he lifted her down as though she was as light as a feather. He slowly lowered her to the ground, allowing her body to brush against the length of his.

That action sent the fire of her desire spreading through her. She gazed up at him through her wind-tousled hair. "You're not playing fair," she said in a nearly inaudible tone. She held on to his arms, admiring the strength in them. Her body was so close to his that she could feel his bulging arousal against her feminine mound, causing her to grow moist with desire. She was enthralled by the way she felt and cursed herself for the way her body had betrayed her, causing her to toss all of her common sense to the wind.

"Who's playing, angel?" He locked his hands at the small of her back and gave her a deep, passionate kiss.

Jenny submitted to the honey-flavored kiss. Sexual desire clouded her mind. His tongue separated her lips and probed the inside of her mouth. Her knees weakened from the heady sensation of his tongue rolling around hers. Her resolve melted. She wrapped her arms around his neck and returned his affection with equal ardor. His unrelenting affection, his attention, radiated boundless excitement within her. Feeling the hem of her dress being lifted, she didn't smack his hand away. She welcomed his caress on her bottom, her thighs. His soothing hand slipped inside her bikini panties, seeking the moist pearl of passion. She let out a sizzling gasp of delight; her head pressed against his shoulders while his long fingers drifted in and out of her wetness. Feeling weak with desire, she gripped handfuls of his shirt to keep from falling to her knees.

Laurence's open mouth was pressed at her neck. He flicked his tongue over her flesh and placed igniting kisses at its base. "I want you so badly. Can...I must have..."

Aching with desire, Jenny responded in a hoarse whisper. "Yes...hmm...oh yes," she said, surrendering to his request.

Laurence backed Jenny to the huge boulder. He unbuckled his slacks and dropped them along with his briefs. While sheathing his firm manhood with a condom, he layered her neck with kisses.

Shoving up her dress to her waist, Laurence lifted her legs and penetrated her with an eager thrust.

The pulsating feel of him inside of her made her feel as though the bones had melted in her body. She wrapped her legs around his thighs and braced her back against the hard, rough edges of the rock.

Laurence clutched her bottom and worked his passion rod with masterful strokes. He kissed her lips; he nibbled them as the intensity of their union mounted.

Jenny's hungry body absorbed the joy she shared with her lover. The sex was raw with unspeakable passion. She moaned and whimpered from all the rapture that Laurence gave her. As her temperature and pleasure-point rose, she grabbed hold of the back of his neck. The fire of her climax coursed from the core of her, dazzling her and causing her to unleash a loud moan, which mingled with the roar of the ocean.

"Hold on," Laurence grunted. He locked his hands at her bottom and proceeded to thrust with a ferocity that caused him to peak and her to find the rapture of yet another release.

At the end of their love journey, they dropped to the sand and held each other, allowing the ocean breeze to cool the fever of their passion.

Laurence cupped Jenny's chin and placed a wet kiss on her eyelids, the tip of her nose, then her now-swollen lips. He moaned as though he had tasted something wonderful.

She rested her head on his shoulder to nibble and kiss his neck. She sighed, loving the way her body seemed to hum from her titillation.

Deep within her soul, she hoped that what had happened was more than just sex. She had not only given him her body but also a piece of her heart as well. She hadn't meant for that to happen. It just did. She knew that if she wasn't careful she could be in jeopardy of setting herself up for heartache. Again. Down on the beach on this beautiful night she was the woman of Laurence's dreams. But who knew how Laurence would be with the dawn of a new day, or on their return to the real world in Harper Falls?

***

As the new day dawned, Jenny felt drugged by the romance and passion of the evening.

By the time she and Laurence had returned from their beach interlude, she was glad that he had invited her to his room. She didn't want to be alone, feeling as glorious as she did. She had given herself to him shamelessly and he had pleasured her divinely. She had no regrets. Jenny wasn't naive enough to believe that love had anything to do with what had occurred. She realized it was only a sexual thing. And that was enough for her right now. She rationalized it as a form of therapy. She needed to be touched and held, to feel the kind of passion he had incited in her.

She had pretended to be numb for too long.

In the privacy of his suite, Jenny awoke nude, resting face down on Laurence's bed. All of a sudden he straddled her, causing her to giggle. She relished the thrill of his steel-like essence brushing against her back. His strong hands massaged and caressed her back and shoulders and his thumbs pressed along her spine to soothe her soul. She fantasized the world the way it could be, if she were the woman he wanted as his. When Laurence fell away from her, she rolled toward him so that he could enfold her in his arms.

"Am I dreaming?" she asked softly, sliding her arms around his waist.

He licked her earlobe, kissed it and breathed deeply. "If it is a dream, I don't want to wake up," he said, moving on top of her.

Once again she grew hungry for him. She tasted his lips and moved to his neck, causing him to sigh. She held his hot body to hers, growing more intoxicated by his wonderful maleness.

Hugging her to him, Laurence sighed; he kissed her fervently. He cupped one of her breasts and rolled its nipple between his forefinger and thumb until it swelled from his teasing touch. Jenny felt the sensation in her love haven. She arched her body upward and offered her other breast to him.

Without hesitation, Laurence sucked the pouted tip slowly. His hand wandered to the soft hair of her passion flower and caressed the inner lips, electrifying the core.

As currents of desire spiraled through her, Jenny moaned. She pressed her thighs together around his hand to hold onto the exquisite feeling. His skillful fingers made her swoon. She swirled her hips against the delightful pressure of his busy fingers. He took her to the precipice of ecstasy, then removed his fingers. He moved on top of her to fill her with his swollen, condom-sheathed rod. His thrusts were full of an immediacy that set her body into a wondrous rhythm to match the beating of her heart. The rapture of their joined bodies was splendid. She groaned loudly in celebration. She locked her legs around his waist and rocked him wildly.

Her uninhibited surrender to Laurence set his pulse racing and turned his blood to liquid fire. Growling, he unleashed his passion. Lost in the hot, sticky web of her haven, he set to stroking deeper and harder. Panting as hard as he was from their love labor, he silenced himself by tasting her luscious hard nipples. Soon the tasting of her breasts and his steady thrusting began to take him to the crest of his climax.

Much to Jenny's chagrin, she couldn't endure the powerful sensations any longer. She simply couldn't hold out. She dug her nails into Laurence's shoulder; her panting, ascending to loud groans, alerted him to the advent of her orgasm.

He gripped her wildly pumping bottom and held his face next to hers. He thrust harder and faster until, like her, he too came in a body-shuddering climax that caused him to call out her name as though she had saved his life.

In the afterglow of their intimacy, they lay close together in a spooned position. Laurence's face was against her soft, sweaty hair and his arms were locked around her waist. Before he drifted off to sleep, he was barely able to tell her how great it had been.

Just sex, Jenny reminded herself ruefully. Still, she liked the feel of his strong arms and body, warming her flesh. It was heavenly being with him. She covered his interlocked hands at her waist with hers. Then she too fell asleep, relishing the way her being felt as though it was glowing from the sweet encounters she had shared all through the night.

Jenny was startled out of her sleep by a pounding upon Laurence's door. She looked at the clock and noticed that it was ten a.m..

Laurence bolted upright in bed. "Who in the hell can that be?" He glared at the door, clearly resenting the intrusion.

A male voice shouted in a humorous tone. "Laurence, man, get your butt in gear and open the door."

Swearing, Laurence rolled out of bed and jumped to his feet. He hustled into the bathroom and returned with two terrycloth bathrobes. He flung one at Jenny, then slipped into the other. "It's Roscoe Baker," he said in a hushed tone. "I completely forgot he said he was coming by this morning." He slapped his forehead with the heel of his hand. "The bathroom. Go. Stay there until I can get rid of him."

Scrambling out of the tangled sheets, Jenny covered herself with the robe. She didn't want Mr. Baker to find her with Laurence any more than her boss did. As she hurried out of the room, Laurence stuffed her clothes in her arms and kicked her sandals under the bed.

Inside the bathroom, Jenny dressed quietly. She stared at her face in the mirror and noticed how her light complexion glowed radiantly. Her lips looked sensual—swollen from the nibbling kisses of her new-found lover. Leaning her head to the side and lifting her hair off her neck, she spotted a reddish mark. A passion mark. She blushed at the badge from her intense coupling. She had never imagined Laurence to be such a sweet, passionate man. A shiver went up her spine, remembering how he had made her whole soul and heart rejoice.

Hearing the two men laughing and talking, Jenny went to the bathroom door and cracked it enough to hear them conversing. She wanted to see if Laurence had persuaded Roscoe to leave.

She was starving and ready for a hearty break- fast, which she hoped to share with Laurence.

"You tiger, you've had a one-nighter. Look at that bed! I know that scene." Roscoe laughed. "I'm glad you've gotten yourself a piece. I was wondering when you were going to end that dry spell of yours. Virginia Beach is the place, man. The women here are gorgeous and sensual, and in the summer they are always strutting around in next to nothing on the beaches.

It's a male paradise. It's exactly where a stressed-out man like yourself needs to be. A man who hasn't taken the time to be with a woman in who knows when."

Jenny heard Laurence laughing nervously with his friend. She was pleased that he hadn't given up the name of his mystery lover.

"How are things going with you and that dumb, sexy assistant you brought along with you?" Roscoe asked. "She's the kind of woman that you want only to open her legs and not her mouth. You were right, Laurence, when you said she isn't the brightest woman. Like you said, she was good enough to answer the phone and to write down messages." He chuckled. " I don't know why you're holding on to her. She nearly ruined you with that mix-up of materials. She's shown you how inept she is. But then I suppose she's a pleasant decoration to have around. I know I'd be as inspired and creative as you, to see a behind like hers wriggling and jiggling at my office. It sort of relieves the tension of the workplace, huh?"

Glancing toward the bathroom door, Laurence noticed that it was partly opened. He wished he could disappear. He hoped she hadn't heard the thoughtless and cruel comments that he had made out of frustration to Roscoe one day. What had been said was way before he had had the opportunity to get to know and understand Jenny. And then he had been edgy ever since he had had to return to Harper Falls. Knowing that his father didn't appreciate the sacrifice he had made by coming to be with him, Laurence had experienced all the old insecurities and inadequacies he had had to deal with, involving his old man.

"Enough, man," Laurence said. "Don't talk about the lady like that. I was certainly wrong," he said, hoping she heard this. "She has grown. She's turning into quite a professional. She's a hard worker. She just needed time to learn things and to work with a sourpuss like myself."

Roscoe remained silent for a moment. "Hmm...I wonder what could have possibly brought on your change of heart. Has a tumble in the sheets with her brought on this change of attitude?"

Jenny wished she could vaporize from all she was hearing. She watched Laurence stride to the door and open it. "I hate to rush you. But I've got things to do, man."

Roscoe gave a lecherous laugh. "Sure. Fine, man. I'm out of here. I've got a pretty young thing waiting on me. You aren't the only one who has gotten lucky. Hey, why don't you join us for breakfast? That's why I came anyway. My date has a friend who is ideal for you. I'll give you a call, okay?"

Laurence stood at the door, looking impatient. "No, thanks, man. I have some things to do. Business to be taken care of."

"Well, I'll call you later anyway. Maybe you will have changed your mind and decided to hang out with me." Roscoe ambled out of the room.

Laurence slammed the door and stood staring into space, trying to figure out how to put a positive spin on all that Roscoe had said negatively, concerning Jenny.

Jenny softly closed the bathroom door after Roscoe had left. She stood, feeling embarrassed and used. Hearing that Baker man repeat the things Laurence had said, Jenny realized she had been seduced for her boss's pleasure. She had already figured that their relationship was just sexual. But to know that she'd been used for entertainment only was a whole different thing. She bet the first chance Laurence got he was going to fill Roscoe in on all the erotic details of their whirlwind tumble in bed.

A reluctant rap on the bathroom door broke her reverie. "Jenny, you can come out. It's all clear," he said in a gentle tone.

Jenny didn't answer. She didn't want to come out and face him. She stared at herself in the mirror and hated the tears that pooled in her eyes. She blinked them back and swallowed hard. She tried hard not to submit to the tears of shame that burned her eyes. She breathed deeply and opened the door.

Returning to the bedroom, Jenny found Laurence dressed in only a pair of jeans. Though he looked yummy, she couldn't look at him for long. She dropped to her knees to retrieve her sandals from under the bed. All the while she didn't say a word to Laurence. She stood up, shoving one foot then the other into her shoes.

Observing her, Laurence was disturbed by her silence and that shrinking-violet look of hers. He hadn't seen it since she had charmed him after the incident with Chloe. It bothered him to see her with slumped shoulders, looking as though she wished she were invisible.

"You can't leave without breakfast. I'll call room service. Just tell me what you'd like," he said in a too-cheery tone.

He noticed that the glow he had seen earlier in her eyes, from their grand night of passion, had vanished. His heart fell along with the genuine joy he'd experienced with her in his arms, loving him and making him feel more complete than he ever had.

Laurence went to her and took hold of her shoulders, but Jenny wouldn't meet his gaze.

He placed a finger beneath her chin and tilted her face toward his. "You heard that junk Roscoe was talking, didn't you? I know you did. I saw the cracked door." His tone was apologetic.

She swiped away his hand and stepped away from him. "I wasn't snooping. I was only listening to see when he would leave. And I happened to hear some interesting things."

Laurence's brow furrowed. He didn't like her resisting his touch. He rubbed the side of his face thoughtfully; he stared at Jenny to figure out what to say.

In her sensitive mood, Jenny mistook Laurence's look as arrogance and her face flushed with shame that quickly turned to fury. "I had no idea that I had been the butt of your private jokes with your friends," she said. Thinking of what she had heard, her body grew rigid with indignation.

Laurence tried to remain civil. He eased toward his lover, who had grown cold. "My apologies. You see, I'm not used to working or being around women who aren't assertive or who second-guess themselves. With the kind of work I do, I have to be stern and straightforward. If I weren't that way, people would walk all over me and I'd have no business or career." He stared at her, hoping she would see his point. "You aggravated me when you first came to work for me. I couldn't figure what was up with all the shyness and reluctance on your part. I'd hired you as a favor to a friend. Though you didn't have the qualifications, I thought sure you'd work out for me. In the beginning, things were shaky. But you've grown. You're going to be all right, now that you aren't scared of me anymore." He stepped toward her and reached out to take her in his arms.

Jenny stepped away from him. His words hadn't eased her hurt. She still wasn't ready to forget those awful things that had been said about her. She glared up at him. "I won't be your lover anymore. And I don't want to work for you, either. Last night, this morning—all of it was just one more mistake in my life."

Disappointment filled Laurence's eyes. "Wait a minute, Jenny. You don't have to give up your job. And don't say that what we shared isn't special. I know you're hurt. But you have no reason to be. I care about you. I really do."

She shrugged to hide her confusion. She wanted to forgive him, but her pride was at stake. She couldn't allow herself to be thought of as just a mindless, sweet lay. She'd had enough men disrespect her. No more. Laurence was much more clever and sophisticated than the others who had used her, but still she knew the trap could be the same one that all the others had set for her. Hadn't he talked about her to his friend as though she wasn't anything?

She whirled away from his intense stare and headed for the door.

Laurence blocked her way. "Jenny, please don't walk out angry. Certainly, we can work through this." He gave her a weak smile, hoping that he could eradicate her anger. "I suppose I'm no match for those romance heroes you read about."

Jenny gave him a defiant look. "No, you sure aren't." She reached around him for the doorknob.

Laurence had no choice but to step aside and allow her to leave.

Outside and away from Laurence, Jenny strutted toward her room at the end of the hallway. As she neared it, her steps faltered. She considered rushing back to Laurence and falling into his arms. She didn't want to believe that a man who had been so loving and tender would one day end up being the devil in disguise. Hadn't she learned from her women's support group that abuse could be found in men from all social groups? Despite what she knew, she wished that she and Laurence could have made it as lovers. She hated herself for wanting him. She tried to tell herself that she was fortunate to overhear the conversation. How in the world was a working-class person like herself supposed to fit into the glamorous world of Laurence Strong? If Roscoe Baker, one of his friends, had ridiculed her, she was certain that his other peers would be just as cruel to her. Jenny decided it was best that she take her head out of the clouds. It was best that she continue to get her romance vicariously through her reading, she decided. It was certainly safer. Much safer to live in a fantasy world.

After Jenny left, Laurence went to the mini-bar and poured himself a drink of scotch. It didn't matter to him that it wasn't noon yet. How dare Jenny dismiss their interlude? Maybe he had been wrong for making his move on her at this place. It made it seem as though he had brought her along only for his sexual convenience. He gulped his drink and welcomed its warmth. He closed his eyes and remembered how hot and silky her skin had been to his touch. He needed another drink when he thought of how sweetly and passionately her body had cradled his, lost in rapture. Jenny Martin was as exciting and sensual as he had imagined her. While he was with her, he believed that she genuinely cared for him. This was a rarity for him. Since he had become successful and wealthy, he had encountered many shallow and superficial women, most of whom had an agenda. They wanted to be with him because they felt being with him would be like winning a lottery. He refused to be any woman's prize that way. He would rather live alone than be thought of only as a checkbook.

But Jenny Martin had touched his heart. She was down to earth, yet complicated. He had ruined his chances with her with his thoughtless remarks to that mouthy Roscoe Baker. Had he known that he would fall for her, he certainly wouldn't have said the things he had. Now she wanted nothing to do with him. She had quit her job. She was out of his life. But he wasn't ready to give up on her. He needed her. He believed that if she allowed him in her life, he could know what it was to love her and himself again.

He was intrigued by Jenny, who had experienced so much unpleasantness in her life. He was anxious to know how a woman like herself found the strength and the courage to go on. He had two hurdles in his own life that he hadn't been able to cross. The loss of his brother and the anguish of trying to win his father's affection. He had hoped that Jenny's love and support would strengthen

him to face these demons in his life. He poured
himself another drink and gulped it down. Jenny
had quit her job, but he refused to let her out of his
heart.

Chapter 8

Jenny walked into the Martin L. King Elementary School, past the vibrant autumn leaves, feeling pleased with how Chloe was doing in her new grade. She was even more proud that not only had her daughter's artwork been chosen to go on display, but also that the art teacher had decided that one of Chloe's drawings would be used on a t-shirt for the school's fund-raiser. The drawing was of the teddy bear that Laurence had given her. The one that Chloe affectionately called Cuddly Berry Bear.

When the principal, Mrs. Mays, called Chloe to the stage to receive her certificate for her accomplishment along with a gift certificate, Jenny moved out of her seat to take a picture of the event. She managed to click two pictures of her Chloe. As she returned to her seat, Jenny caught a glimpse of Laurence Strong. He stood in back of the auditorium, standing out from the rest of the parents, wearing a green sweater. Her gaze met his and for a moment she felt as though time had frozen. It had been almost four months since the convention. She hadn't seen Laurence since then.

What in the world was he doing here? she wondered, taking her seat and trying to compose herself. She directed her attention to the stage where
Chloe, along with the other second and third
graders, was singing a song to close out the program. Jenny found it difficult concentrate. Without
looking over her shoulder, she knew that Laurence
was watching her. She grew warm and ill-at-ease
that he had now shown up in her world. She was
tempted to glance his way. Though unwelcome, the
sight of him had been quite appealing. He was a
stunning man. Flashes of their night of passion
flickered in her mind. But the beauty of the evening
had been quickly marred by the cruel things she
had heard he said about her.

Suddenly, the program was over and the audi-
ence burst into applause. An announcement was
made that the children's artwork would be on display in the cafeteria, where refreshments were also
being served.

Seeing an excited Chloe march up the aisle
toward her, Jenny stood up and prepared to give
her daughter a congratulatory hug. She grabbed
Chloe's hand and embraced her. "I'm so proud of
you. I've got pictures, baby," she told her daughter,
who squirmed in her arms to break her mother's
loving embrace.

"Mommy, he's here. He came," Chloe said with
delight, staring down the aisle.

Jenny followed her daughter's gaze. Chloe left her to rush up to Laurence. She took his hand and started towing him toward her mother.

Jenny cursed silently. She wasn't ready to confront Laurence. The final time they had spoken had been to make arrangements for him to mail her the last paycheck that was due her.

"Mommy, Mr. Strong wanted to say hello to you," Chloe said. "Then he wants me to show him the rest of my pictures in the cafeteria."

Laurence stared at Jenny. The expression in his tawny eyes seemed to plead for friendship.

Jenny was cool, yet friendly. She didn't want Chloe to know the depth of her displeasure with Laurence. She had told her daughter that she had left her job because she missed working with her friends at Wal-Mart. It was an excuse that her seven-year-old had bought without question. At Chloe's age, friends were important and worth sacrificing everything for, even a good-paying job with health benefits.

Jenny said, "Hello, how are you? You're the last person I expected to see at a P.T. A. meeting." She rubbed her neck, hoping the heat she experienced being near him wasn't reflected on her face.

Laurence gave her an easy smile. "I have to admit that I feel out of place. This isn't my kind of scene. But when Chloe called and invited me, I couldn't refuse to come and see her work."

Jenny swung her gaze to her daughter and gave her a questioning look.

The child's eyes widened. "Mommy, Mr. Strong gave me Cuddly Berry Bear. And he always told me I was an artist. I wanted him to see me get my prize and to see the t-shirts, too. We're going to buy him one, aren't we? I told him you would," she said in a whiny tone.

Laurence chuckled. "You didn't know she had invited me," he said to Jenny.

"I had no idea," Jenny said, studying her daughter with a tinge of anger that was reluctantly replaced by amusement.

"In that case, I won't make you buy me a t-shirt. Since this is a fund raiser, I'll buy my own along with several others," he volunteered, patting Chloe on the head.

"C'mon, let's get to the cafeteria before everyone eats up all the cookies," Chloe said, taking her mother and Laurence by the hand to lead them to the exhibit.

On their way down the hall, Chloe's young-looking teacher, Miss Goines, stopped them.

"Mr. Martin, Mrs. Martin, I know you both are proud of your little girl. She is quite talented," she said, beaming at Chloe.

Before Jenny could clear up the fact that Laurence wasn't Chloe's father, Miss Goines was beckoned by another teacher.

Chloe giggled and stared up at Laurence. "She thinks you are my daddy."

Laurence's eyes glinted with amusement.

Jenny saw no humor in the incident. "We're going to have to clear that up the first chance we get," she told her daughter. "It's not right to have her believe Mr. Strong is your father."

"It's no big deal," Laurence said. "I would be proud to have a bright little girl like Chloe."

Reaching the cafeteria, Jenny sighed with resignation. She couldn't believe the awkward situation her own daughter had placed her in.

Chloe's picture of the teddy bear was on display along with three other pieces of her work.

Laurence studied the artwork and grinned with approval. "Chloe, these are all excellent!" he gushed, beaming at the child.

Chloe's brown face grew radiant from his compliment. "Thank you," she said in a bashful manner.

"I told you you had an artist on your hands," Laurence said to Jenny.

Jenny nodded in agreement. "I always thought she was exceptional."

Spotting some of her classmates at the refreshment table, Chloe wandered off from the two adults to join them.

With Chloe gone, Laurence turned to Jenny, who had kept her conversation to a minimum with him. "I know you are proud of her," he said, watching Chloe laughing and talking with her friends. "Just think. If she is this good now, what she will do as she gets older? Was her father artistic, too?"

Jenny remembered how Chloe's late father, Willie, could recreate the images of the comic books he read, using only a ballpoint pen or pencil on notebook paper. She had never thought of it as a special talent, but she supposed he was creative, to get them as perfect as he had. "Yes...yes, he was," she said.

As the crowd in the cafeteria thinned out and Chloe's friends left with their parents one by one, Chloe dashed over to her mother and Laurence. "Mommy, are we still going for pizza?"

Jenny glanced at her watch; it was nearly eight o'clock. "It's near your bedtime. But I suppose we can make an exception for tonight."

Chloe glanced at Laurence, beaming. "You can come, too," she said.

Jenny forced a smile. "Chloe, Mr. Strong is a busy man. He probably has something else to do, baby," she said, trying to let Laurence know in a subtle way that she didn't want his company.

Chloe looked disappointed and gave Laurence a sad-eyed look.

Laurence seemed pleased that Chloe hadn't made it so easy for her mother to get rid of him.

"You know, I don't have any plans. I'd loved to have pizza with our little celebrity," he said innocently.

Jenny gave Laurence a critical squint. "Well, we'd better leave. Mr. Strong can follow us to the restaurant in his car." She took Chloe by the hand and stormed toward the exit.

"Mommy, why are you walking so fast?" Chloe asked, looking back for Laurence.

"He can catch up," Jenny said, seething at her predicament.

***

At Gino's restaurant, Laurence and Chloe heartily ate the large pizza loaded with two toppings and extra cheese. Jenny hardly had any appetite. She only wanted to get away from Laurence, who had somehow utterly charmed her daughter. She suddenly wondered how many times Chloe had spoken to Laurence behind her back. She knew the child had memorized his number, because Jenny had insisted she do so when she was working for him.

She watched them enjoying each other's company, telling one another silly jokes. She was surprised to see Laurence rid himself of his serious personality. He seemed to be quite at ease with Chloe now. Gone was that uptight expression he once had had Jenny had to bring Chloe to the office. She wondered what had caused him to make such a complete change. Was he using her daughter to get next to Jenny, to get her back into bed with him? she mused. If he was, he was fighting a losing battle. She wasn't about to get drawn into his web of deception.

"Chloe, it's getting late. We should be leaving. You have school tomorrow," she reminded the child.

Chloe wiped her mouth. "I have to use the bathroom first." She slid out of the booth and skipped toward the restroom.

"I have really enjoyed this evening. Chloe is a delight," Laurence said, smiling at Jenny. His eyes sparkled with the mirth he had shared with Chloe.

"She's had fun, too," Jenny said, unable to bear his eyes or his smile. She kept telling herself not to give in to their charm.

"So, how are things at Wal-Mart?" he asked.

She glared at him to see if he was making fun of her. "They're fine. It's like going home for me."

Laurence shook his head. "Jenny, don't be stubborn. You can have your job back. I won't attack you. I know that you have only been working there part-time and that you've taken another job telemarketing."

Jenny gasped with indignation. "Who told you this?"

Laurence gave her a sympathetic look. "It doesn't matter. I only want to help you. There's no need for you to be running around like a maniac, trying to make ends meet, when you can be making more, working for me."

"I didn't ask for your help. I'm doing just fine," she said, hating the pitying look she saw.

He reached across the table and covered her hand with his. "Jenny, what will I have to do to make you forget those awful things you heard? How can I convince you that I meant no disrespect to you when we went away?"

The warmth of his hand on hers zapped her heart and caused it to flutter with emotions she had been struggling with all evening. It took everything in her to keep from turning her hand over to grip his hand in a display of affection. Instead, she snatched it away and ignored his offer.

She stood. "I better check on Chloe. I bet she's playing in the water while she's washing her hands." She looked in the direction of the restroom.

Laurence jumped to his feet and stood before her. "I'm not giving up on you," he warned her. "Thanksgiving is in a few weeks. Why won't you let me take you and Chloe somewhere nice for dinner?"

Jenny looked over his shoulder to see her daughter finally saunter from the restroom. The front of her shirt was soaked with water. She left

Laurence standing. "Girl, what have I told you about playing in the water?" she snapped angrily. "Let's get your coat and go home." Her brow furrowed with annoyance.

Laurence stood by helplessly, watching Jenny put Chloe into her coat. "What about Thanksgiving?" he asked again. "I know Chloe would love going to a restaurant."

Jenny swung her gaze to Laurence. "I can't. Chloe and I are going out of town," she answered sharply.

"We're going to fly to Chicago," Chloe said with excitement. "We're going to Aunt Nina's and Uncle Addison's."

Jenny wanted to place her hand over her child's mouth for giving away her plans. She didn't want Laurence to know any of her personal business.

"Oh, I see. Well, that's great," he said slowly. He directed his attention to Chloe. "Have you ever been on an airplane?"

"No, I haven't. I can't wait," Chloe said.

Jenny grabbed Chloe by the hand. "Well, it was nice seeing you again. Thanks for taking an interest in Chloe and her program," she said in a cool tone and led Chloe out of the restaurant.

Watching Jenny leave, Laurence dropped back into his seat, feeling forlorn and rejected.

He managed a smile for Chloe, who had turned to wave, giving him a look that was as confused as he felt.

Chapter 9

Sitting at the Thanksgiving dinner table with Nina and Addison in their luxurious Chicago apartment, Jenny knew she had every reason to feel blessed. She was grateful that her friends had paid for her and Chloe's flight so that they could share the holiday with them. However, Jenny couldn't stop thinking of Laurence Strong. She wondered how and with whom he was spending his day. When she had seen him a few weeks ago, she had been downright cold and rude toward him. She wished that she had set her bad feelings aside that evening—he had taken time to come and see Chloe's work at the P.T.A. meeting. The moment she had seen him, she had been hit by the tender affections she harbored for him. She had believed that her emotions for such a successful man could never go beyond being a fantasy. But seeing him unexpectedly that evening, she had been caught off guard. She had felt that she had to beat down her fond feelings by treating him cruelly. She knew that she had probably smothered any feelings that he might have had for her. But that was good, she figured. She had saved herself from any further heartache and disappointment. She still hadn't got-

ten over the humiliation of the convention weekend.

Nina tapped Jenny on her hand to bring her out
of her reverie. "Jenny, hello. A penny for your
thoughts," Nina teased.

Jenny blinked at Nina; she had forgotten where
she was. "Oh, I'm sorry."

Nina studied her friend with interest. "What is
on your mind, girl? You're not yourself. Is there
anything you want to talk about?"

Jenny sighed and glanced at Addison, who was
looking as concerned as his wife.

"I'm okay. I suppose I'm just tired," she said.

Addison leaned toward Jenny and pointed his
finger. "See, if you had continued to work for
Laurence, you wouldn't be running around, trying
to hold down two jobs."

"Addison, leave her alone. It didn't work out for
her," Nina said.

"I haven't understood that. Why is it that it did-
n't?"

"I'd rather not talk about that now. This is supposed to be a pleasant occasion," Jenny said.

Addison gave Nina a questioning look.
"Laurence is a good guy. He might be a bit stressed.
He's operating two offices. I ran into him the other
day. He's in town for a few days, clearing up a few
things. He had to attend a ribbon-cutting for that

new wing of the children's hospital here that he designed."

Jenny nearly choked on her food. "Laurence is here in Chicago?" She thought of what a coincidence it was for him to be in town at the same time that she was.

Addison look amused. "He sure is. You have to remember he considers Chicago his home. He's only in Harper Falls to keep tabs on his stubborn old man. Oh, by the way, I invited him by for some holiday cheer. You know how lonely bachelors get around the holidays."

"That was nice of you, Addison. You didn't mention this to me," Nina said dryly, seeing how out of sorts Jenny was upon hearing this information.

"You had me so busy with kitchen chores that I forgot. Besides, I knew you wouldn't mind." He winked at his wife.

Chloe had finished her dinner and sat in her seat, squirming. "Are we still going to the movies?"

"Of course we are," Nina said. "As soon as we clear away the dishes and place them in the dishwasher."

Jenny noticed Nina and Addison exchanging a secret look. Addison grinned at Nina and nodded.

"Okay, what's up, you guys?" Jenny asked, sensing that there was something more to be told.

"Addison and I have some good news to share with you," Nina said. Her eyes twinkled with joy. "I'm pregnant," she gushed.

Jenny jumped from her seat to hug Nina. "That's wonderful. I'm so happy for you."

She went to Addison and shoved his shoulder playfully. "Congratulations."

"A baby!" Chloe exclaimed. "Can I be your babysitter?" She grinned at Nina and stared at the woman's stomach as though she could see the baby growing.

"When you get a bit older, sweetheart," Nina said. "But I'm going to need you to help me look after it when it comes." She squeezed Chloe on the cheek.

The doorbell rang, interrupting their excited chatter about the new baby.

"That must be Laurence," Addison said, staring at Jenny with an amused look. He left the table to get the door.

Jenny attempted to move out of her seat and leave the room.

Nina shook her head at Jenny. "Don't. There's no reason for you to be rude," she chided.

Returning to the dining room, Addison was followed by Laurence Strong.

"Happy Thanksgiving, everyone," Laurence said cheerily. His gaze fell on Jenny and lingered.

Though she greeted him with a tight-lipped smile, her face brightened briefly.

Nina smiled. "Happy Thanksgiving to you, Laurence. It's so nice of you to come by. We were ready to have dessert. Have a seat and join us." She rose from her seat to clear away the dinner dishes.

"Mr. Strong, you followed us to Chicago," Chloe declared, kneeling in her seat and grinning at her friend, who took the empty chair beside her.

"No, I didn't exactly follow you. I've been here for a while. I had work to do, sweetheart. You must have followed me, kiddo." He tweaked her nose.

Addison assisted his wife with the dishes. "Come on, Chloe. Help us serve dessert," he suggested.

"I can help," Jenny volunteered, rising half out of her seat.

"No, you stay and keep Laurence company," Nina insisted, following Addison and Chloe into the kitchen.

Jenny had mixed feelings about being left alone with Laurence. She knew that though she had distanced herself from him she still had tender feelings for the man. And she knew that in her vulnerable state she could be easily charmed by him, enough to forget all the horrid things he had said behind her back. The last thing she wanted was to be belittled by any man and especially Laurence. Yet secretly she was flattered that he had tracked her down and plotted to get her alone. There was no doubt in her mind that Addison had had a hand in setting up this moment in which she was alone with Laurence. Obviously, Laurence had given Addison enough information about their quarrel to get his assistance. She would have to deal with Laurence one on one. "Small world. Imagine you being here in town the same time that we are," she said in a sarcastic tone.

"Well, I was here before you. Remember, this town is really my home and the place where I started my business," he informed her.

"You never mentioned that you were coming here when I saw you," she said in a hushed tone. She didn't want Nina and Addison to hear.

"You never gave me a chance to say much of anything. You had such a big chip on your shoulder," he countered.

Jenny grew silent and lowered her eyes. She wished that everyone would return to the room soon. She could feel Laurence's watchful stare; it was making her feel uncomfortable.

"Jenny, you and I need to talk. You have treated me like a pervert long enough," he said in a firm tone.

"You hurt me, Laurence. Since my divorce, you were the first man that I had slept with. Our intimacy was special. Can you imagine how I felt when I overheard Roscoe repeating all that stuff you had said about me?" Her anger lit her eyes. "It ruined all the tender feelings and hope I thought we could have for a relationship. But maybe I was wrong to ever dare to think that you'd want me as anything but a one-night stand."

Laurence leaned toward her and gave her an apologetic look. "I'd give anything in the world to take back those things that you heard. But all I can do is to say I'm sorry." He took her reluctant hand and gazed at her. "Jenny," he said softly. "I care for you more than I've cared for any woman in a long time. You have to believe me. I've been in hell ever since you shut me out of your life. Let me talk to you later and maybe I can convince you of how I really feel for you."

Jenny's heart melted with his words. She met his eyes and found them full of genuine sincerity. She squeezed his hand and welcomed the feel of his fingers intertwining with hers. She decided to give him a chance to redeem himself. However, she wasn't going to let him off the hook so easily without letting him know how badly he had made her feel.

Before any more could be said between them, Nina, Addison, and Chloe returned to the room, laughing, to deliver the dessert of pie and ice cream.

As they savored their dessert, Laurence and Jenny exchanged longing looks.

Once dessert was completed, Chloe asked, "Is it time to go to the movie now?"

"It sure is," Addison said. "We have to leave in a few minutes or else we'll miss the beginning of the movie."

Nina said, "Jenny, why don't you stay and visit with Laurence? Addison and I look forward to having Chloe all to ourselves."

Chloe went to her mother and draped an arm around her shoulder. "I thought Mommy was going with us. Mr. Strong can go with us too, can't he?"

Nina took Chloe by the hand to ease her out of the room to find her things for their movie engagement. "She can go with us next time. We'll see another movie tomorrow."

Jenny gave Nina an appreciative look. She knew her friend knew her well enough to see that the difficulty she had had with Laurence was being resolved. She imagined that her face revealed the positive change of emotions she had had.

Once Nina and Addison had left with a loquacious Chloe, Jenny prepared coffee to serve in the living room with Laurence.

The fireplace had a cozy fire burning. Jenny found Laurence standing and admiring the hearth. Her glimpse of him, dressed in jeans and a denim shirt with a sport coat, reminded her of why she had found him so intriguing. Not only was he bright, but he was great looking in whatever he wore.

"Coffee," Jenny announced, settling the tray on the table.

Laurence smiled at her and joined her on the sofa, where she served him.

"So, where should we begin our conversation?" she asked in an encouraging tone.

Laurence took a sip of his coffee, then set it aside. He rested his hands on his knees and gazed at her. "The main thing that I want to convey to you is that I have a lot of respect for you. When you first came to work for me, I have to admit that I had my doubts about your work ability. And I did make some disparaging comments about you to my friend, Roscoe. I was wrong. But if you remember correctly, that day was a hectic and horrible day. I had job issues and family issues that I was dealing with."

Jenny held his gaze with interest. "Still, it doesn't excuse the things you said about me. You knew that I didn't have much experience when you hired me. I did the best I could when I came to work. I could have done much better had you not barked at me or intimidated me with your arrogance," she said in a chiding tone.

His face flushed with embarrassment. "Okay, I admit that I was a bit harsh. But that's me when I'm stressed or under deadline to complete a job.

That's business. But I have to remember that people who live in Harper Falls have to be coddled." He eyed her with a chastened look.

"There you go. You're talking down to me again," Jenny said accusingly. Her lips twitched with annoyance.

His handsome face clouded. "No, you're taking it the wrong way." He took her hand.

"Jenny, there's no need for you to make this any harder than it has to be. I'm going to be straightforward with you. I'm quite fond of you. I haven't been able to stop thinking of you since...since that time we spent together at the convention." He stroked her hand tenderly and gazed into her eyes. "You can't imagine how crushed I was when you walked out on me and refused to work with me anymore. You made me feel like such a brute."

"I had to leave. I couldn't work for you after the things I heard you had said about me, and the way I had just given in to you. To be honest, I felt like a cheap whore. I had no business going all the way with you."

"Oh, no," Laurence said. "You mustn't feel that way. I never thought of you in that light. I'll always remember that night as something that was special. We were two lonely people who found comfort in each other." His face took on a soft, romantic look.

Jenny's heart turned over at his admission. She was touched by his obvious sincerity and honesty. She covered his hand and spoke softly. "I can't believe a man like yourself is lonely."

He gave her a sad smile. "Oh, yes. You just can't imagine how lonely I can get. I may be successful but, believe me, I am no stranger to loneliness." He settled back on the sofa and pulled her next to him.

Jenny didn't resist him. She welcomed his closeness. After hearing his apology, she had no qualms about accepting the brief, tender kiss he gave her. The moment that their lips met, a spark in her heart ignited all the feelings about him that she had ignored these last months. She closed her eyes and tilted her head to welcome more sweet kisses.

Laurence obliged her with ardent, sweet kisses. He gathered her in his arms and held her snugly to him. "Hmm...I thought I'd never get the chance to hold you again," he whispered, his breath hot against her ear.

A rush of desire coursed through Jenny. "I don't want to need you," she said in a regretful tone. All the while she accepted his ardent affection.

Laurence held her so that he could assess her expression. "Why is it that you don't want to need me?"

Jenny disentangled herself from him; she needed to figure out how to word what she had to say.
"Laurence, there are times when you frighten me,"
she said, looking somber.

He looked puzzled. "Frighten you? In what
way?"

"Your temper. I've seen how you can fly off the
handle at work, over issues concerning the firm.
When you do that, it reminds me...it reminds me of
the hell I lived in when I was married. I can't go
back to that. I won't go back to living in fear ever
again."

Laurence moved to the edge of the chair and
stared at her, baffled. "Are you trying to say that
you fear I might be abusive?"

She boldly met his gaze. "I don't want to believe
it. But it's just a gut feeling I have."

He placed an arm around her shoulder. "I
would never hurt you in the way you've been hurt
before. Yes, I have a temper, but I'd never hit a
woman. I'm not some lowlife punk."

Jenny touched his face and stared into his
eyes, finding honesty. "I want to believe you."

He kissed her lips tenderly. "Then believe it.
Give me a chance to show you what kind of a man
I can be to you," he said in a sensual tone that cap-
tivated her.

Jenny slid her arms around his neck and sur-
rendered to his charms. They shared deep, pas-

sionate kisses that led to them reclining on the sofa. Jenny welcomed the feel of Laurence on top of her. She could feel the heat of his body through his clothes. She was also pleasured by the feel of his arousal upon her feminine essence. She ached for him. Yet she had qualms about making love in Nina's home, on her sofa.

Laurence was relentless with his passion for her. Each spot that he touched and kissed weakened her. All the while she was engaged with him, she remembered how wonderful it had been to have him love her, and she yearned to feel that way again. She felt his hand under her sweater. He unfastened her bra, freeing her breasts. His warm hand fondled a breast, then he tasted its swollen nipple. She moaned softly. The feel of his wet lips and forceful tongue made her feel as though her body was burning.

"I want you," Laurence said in a husky tone. He slipped his tongue inside her mouth.

Jenny rubbed her tongue around his. The sensation caused her to throb in the core of her. In that instant, she knew she had to be with him regardless of where they were. She unbuckled his belt and unzipped his slacks.

With a hint of a smile, he raised himself enough for her to tug off his pants along with his briefs, sliding them over his hips. He reached for his wallet and fumbled for a condom to shield his enlarged member.

As she wiggled out of her slacks and panties, Jenny's eyes widened at the sight of his steel. She fell back on the sofa, opened her arms and parted her legs to welcome him to her.

Laurence studied her glistening feminine essence, then sank himself completely within her with a groan of pleasure.

Wrapping her legs around his body, Jenny abandoned herself to him. At once they fell into an exquisite rocking harmony. She felt as though fire was spreading through her as he brought his stomach against hers. In the midst of their intoxicating passion, she cried out in pleasure. She rocked his whole body with her uninhibited, wild gyrations. She ran her hands under his shirt and over the rippling movements of the muscles of his damp, powerful back. His vitality seeped through her entire body, carrying her to rapturous heights.

Gazing up at Laurence, she felt empowered by the effect she had on him. His eyes were closed, his face contorted, and his teeth were clenched as though he were in sweet agony. Seeing him so, she began to feel strange heats burst inside her, little fires that she was ready to quench. She noticed the way his head fell back and felt his member pulsating inside her. He unleashed a lingering groan, then thrust faster. Locking her arms around his waist, she melted against him, whimpering with all the joy she was experiencing as she felt his honey flow within her. Feeling his body shudder against hers, she strained against him and quivered with a full, joyous climax.

In the afterglow, Laurence lavished her face and neck with wet kisses. He laughed softly and whispered, "Shame on us for making the Wagners' home our love nest." He planted a smacking kiss upon her lips. "I won't tell if you won't." His eyes, drowsy-looking from lovemaking, gazed into hers.

Jenny gave him a satisfied, smoldering smile. "It'll be our little secret," she vowed. She playfully smacked him on his bare bottom.

Chapter 10

After that wonderful romantic interlude with Laurence on Thanksgiving, Jenny's holiday in Chicago was no longer to include Nina, Addison or Chloe. Instead, Laurence encouraged her to spend the next few days with him. He wanted to share his world with her. Jenny was more than willing to oblige him. Once Nina had noticed the radiance on Jenny's face, she encouraged her to make the most of every moment. She assured her that she and Addison would keep Chloe busy enough for Jenny to spend time with Laurence.

The Friday after Thanksgiving, Laurence came by to take Jenny to his opulent office on Michigan Avenue in downtown Chicago. Laurence had a suite of offices that made his Harper Falls office look like a hole in the wall.

"My goodness, this is fantastic. I can understand why you're so restless in Harper Falls," she said after he had given her a tour of his firm and they had returned to his huge office.

"Restless? Is that the way I come across to you?" Laurence asked. He sat on the edge of his mahogany desk, placed his large hands on Jenny's waist and drew her form to him. He gazed at her with a smile in his eyes that contained a sensuous flame.

Placing her hands on his chest, Jenny peered into his eyes with admiration and tender affection. "I used to think of you in more negative terms. But, well, you've convinced me that restless is a more fitting way to define you." She fitted herself between his legs. She buried her face in his neck and inhaled the wonderful scent of his aftershave.

"I have something that I want to ask you," he informed her, caressed her back. He brushed a gentle kiss across her forehead and then gently covered her mouth.

The mastery of his kiss sent a delicious shiver through her. She exhaled to relieve the sexual tension that was settling in the core of her. "What is it that you want to ask me?" Her voice was a low whisper. She had hoped that he would suggest an afternoon of sexual delight on his three-cushioned sofa, which was made of buttery smooth leather. She was more than ready to accept such a proposal. He had informed her that the office was closed for the holiday and no one would show up until Monday.

"I have a dinner to attend at the Marriott on Saturday. Tomorrow. A black tie thing. It's a fraternity event. I'm supposed to present the Man of the Year Award. I want you to go with me," he said. "I want to show you off and introduce you to my friends here."

The request took Jenny by surprise. She stared at him blankly, amazed and very shaken.

She was only beginning to be comfortable with Laurence. But the thought of meeting his friends, who were equally as successful as he, unnerved her. She didn't respond. She moved out of his embrace and over to the window, looking apprehensive.

Laurence came up behind her, slipped his arms around her waist and placed his face next to hers. "Jenny, you haven't answered me. Why the hesitation, baby? I can assure you that you'll have a great time. It's not as stuffy as it might sound."

She whirled around and faced him, wearing a concerned expression. "I...I don't have anything to wear," she said, hoping this would release her from his request. She feared going out socially with him to the kind of event he suggested. She imagined that a woman with a blue collar background like herself would stand out like a sore thumb. She would be miserable around his business associates and society friends.

"Buy something. I'll take you on a shopping spree. You can get whatever you want," he said.

She hadn't counted on that kind of answer. "I–I can't go," she stammered.

Laurence's handsome face clouded with confusion. "Why not? I want you with me. It's going to be a dinner dance. You'll love it. Don't turn me down. I'm always showing up at these things by myself. I usually stay for a short while and then disappear. But this year, I want to spend the entire evening and night with you." He smiled and kissed her briefly on the lips.

Anxiety gripped her. She didn't want to disappoint him. However, she feared going out with him to meet his circle of friends. What could she possibly have in common with these folks? She worked as a clerk in a discount department store and she had been his secretary. She hadn't attended college. She only had a G. E. D. and a few business courses from the community college, and her family background consisted of foster care, a murdered lover who had fathered her daughter, and an abusive ex-husband.

"I'd like to go, Laurence, but I'd rather not. You go on and enjoy yourself," she suggested, hoping he would let the subject go.

"You don't want to be with me," he said, sounding disappointed. He held her hand and stared at her. "You mean the world to me, Jenny. It's been a while since a woman has consumed me the way you have."

The chivalrous words brought a smile to her lips. He was acting as though he was a hero from a romance novel. He had charmed her.

"Okay. I'll go with you," she relented. "But I won't let you buy me an outfit. Nina has things in her closet that I'm sure she'll be more than happy to loan me."

A wave of gratitude washed over his face. He swept Jenny into his arms, lifted her off the floor, kissed her neck and made his way to her lips before lowering her to the floor. Embracing her, he placed his hands on her bottom and began to hustle her toward the sofa. He collapsed there, pulling her down with him.

Jenny giggled with delight. "Mr. Strong, are you planning to seduce me here in this prestigious office of yours?" she teased.

Laurence smiled at her and maneuvered her onto her back. He started to unbutton her blouse. "I sure am. This is something that can't be put off until later."

Her blouse was undone; he nuzzled his face between her warm globes. Jenny was tantalized by his ardent advances, which soon left her aroused and nearly nude.

Laurence fell upon her, joining himself to her with a joyous murmur. His pulsating center of power electrified her. She clung to him and rocked him with all the excitement of the passion she felt for him. Their lovemaking was not the slow or leisurely union they had enjoyed before, but a quick, satisfying pleasure that was full of thrills and sweetness. Straining against each other for kisses and touches here and there, they soon fell into a wondrous rhythm. Soon they were panting and moaning with the rapture that sizzled in their veins. Rolling her body against his, Jenny could feel explosive currents racing through her. Laurence had pushed her bra up to expose her nipples in order to taste them. His tongue caressed them, causing her to arch her body upward.

He gripped her thighs and worked his manly essence in a thrilling, relentless, back and forth motion. Each movement sent her soaring higher, until her peak of delight was reached; she called out his name with her release. Waves of ecstasy throbbed within her as he fell upon her, shuddering until he was spent and satisfied. Sated, he rested upon her body, breathing heavily in her ear. He kissed the side of her face and whispered, "I love you."

Hearing the golden words, Jenny locked her arms around his waist. Tears sprang into her eyes. "Oh, Laurence," she said, touched by his declaration.

He raised himself up to look at her. "Jenny, baby, why the tears?" He wiped them gently away with his fingertips.

"I can't believe that you love me."

"I do. I really do, sweetheart." He smiled and covered her mouth with his in a tender kiss that validated the emotions that he had revealed.

Returning his kisses, she murmured against his lips. "I...I..love...you...too." She hugged him while her heart thumped with all the sentiments she had declared.

***

Jenny returned from her Friday evening date with Laurence, glowing with exuberance. She was glad to find Nina still awake, so that she could tell her about the dance Laurence wanted her to attend.

Nina giggled like a schoolgirl at Jenny's news. "That's wonderful. You and I are the same size. Come on to my room and take a look in my closet. You can wear whatever you want," Nina said, taking Jenny by the hand.

Taking a glimpse of Nina's extensive formal wardrobe in her walk-in closet, Jenny felt as though she was a kid in a toy store. "You pick something out for me. You're used to attending these kinds of affairs," she said, puzzling over what would look appropriate for the evening. "By the way, do you have any courage in here too?" She chuckled. "Not only will I need a good outfit, but I'm going to need a lot of nerve."

Nina shoved racks back and forth and came up with three dresses. "You'll be just fine, Jenny. Just be yourself and you'll be okay," Nina assured her. She displayed the three outfits for Jenny to try on. One was a classy-looking black dress with a split up the front and a glittery top, which Jenny favored.

"This is kind of sassy, huh?" Jenny asked, admiring how sleek and sophisticated she looked in the dress.

Nina walked around Jenny, assessing her. "It's nice, but try this jade one. I want to see how this looks on you," she said, sounding as though she were Jenny's mother.

The moment that Nina saw Jenny dressed in the satiny jade-green number, her eyes lit up with approval. "Oh, Jenny, this is it," she gushed. "You'll look like a princess in that. I love the way it accentuates your shoulders—and you have the perfect bosom for it," Nina said, adjusting the thin straps on her friend's shoulders.

Jenny eyed herself in the mirror and liked what she saw. However, thinking about attending the dance, those I'm-not-good-enough demons cropped up in her mind, robbing her of her enthusiasm. She groaned with anxiety. "Why did I ever agree to go with him? I've never been to any fancy parties like this in my life. I'm so afraid I'll make a fool of myself." She stood with her hands to her face, feeling as though she were on the brink of losing her mind.

Nina stood before her friend and placed a hand on her shoulder. "You're going with him because you care for him. It's obvious that he's crazy over you. It's a simple situation. You should be looking forward to this engagement, not stressing out the way you are."

She gave Nina a helpless look. "I wish you and Addison were going to this thing. It sure would make me feel more at ease. I'm going to stand out like some kind of clod with my small town self." She ran her fingers through her hair and let out a frustrated groan. "I'm not going. I'm going to call him right now and tell him." She whirled away from Nina, marched out of the closet and headed to the telephone in Nina's bedroom.

Nina caught up to her and kept her from using the phone. "Jenny, don't do this. You're not giving yourself a chance," she chided her.

"I'm so afraid. He might get me to that party, start comparing me to all those other glamorous women and realize that I'm only good for one thing."

Nina sat on the side of her bed and pulled Jenny down beside her. "You remind me so much of myself a few years ago when I met Addison. I

used to feel the same way you do. Though I was a
physician, I was still haunted by who I used to be.
You know, that dreary foster care background you
and I both had. For years I always felt inferior
socially. When I met Addison, I was reminded of all
the negative feelings I'd experienced in high school.
He was the handsome hero even then, and I was a
little nobody who had this huge crush on him, just
like every other girl in school. Returning to Harper
Falls to set up my practice, I expected Addison to
be cordial to me and have a clue to who I was, since
we had attended high school together. But he did-
n't remember a thing about me from those days."
Nina sighed and shook her head. "It was all well
and good, I suppose. I was such a pitiful little girl.
But he became interested in me when we had to
work together at the Women's Clinic. I gave him a
hard time. Like you, I was afraid to get involved
with him because he was from this wealthy background. But things worked out for us. We're pretty
happy, even more so now. He can't wait to be a
father." She placed a hand on her stomach, where
her baby was growing.

Jenny tried to be encouraged. She thought of
how different Nina's husband, Addison, was from
Laurence. Addison was an even-natured man.
Laurence was full of stress, and prone to emotion-
al outbursts that still filled her with doubts.
Though he had assured her that he would never do

anything to harm her, she still worried. Hadn't she heard this same promise from her ex-husband, who was a brute?

"Jenny, go to this party. Enjoy yourself. You might as well learn to mingle with his friends. You and he look as though you might have a wonderful future together," Nina said.

With renewed confidence, Jenny rose from the bed and returned to the closet. She selected the black dress she had tried on and held it against herself. "I think I'll wear this tomorrow night. Where are the shoes and bag to match it, kiddo?" She winked at her friend, who was beaming at her.

***

Saturday, the night of Laurence's dinner and dance, Jenny looked as chic as a high-fashion model. Not only had Nina given her clothes to wear, she had also loaned her diamond earrings and a matching necklace. Jenny was flattered by Laurence's reaction to her when he saw her that night. She was touched by the way he placed his hand over his heart and inhaled as though the sight of her took his breath away.

However, arriving at the fraternity dance, she no longer felt as beautiful or special. She noticed the couples getting out of their flashy, expensive cars. The women were gorgeous and sophisticated.

They wore luscious minks or expensive cashmere wraps. The men were handsome and elegant looking. She had never seen so many confident and successful black men and women gathered in one place before. She began to feel like a fish out of a pond. What in the world was she going to say to these people that would be of interest to them?

Laurence took her hand to head to the main ballroom where the event was being held. "Jenny, your hand is as cold as ice," he teased, rubbing it and smiling. "Everything is going to be fine. You look beautiful and I'm proud to be with you," he assured her.

Once they were seated at the reserved table with four other couples and Laurence had introduced her, they had dinner. Jenny relaxed with him at her side.

Laurence leaned over and kissed her on her face. "I'm going to have to leave you for a while. I'm going to mingle with a few of my frat brothers before I make my presentation," he explained.

Jenny gave him a helpless look. Once Laurence left, so did the other guys who had come with their wives or girlfriends. The moment Jenny was alone, the other women eyed her and began to quiz her.

A woman named Miranda asked, "Jenny, dear, how in the world did you manage to hook Laurence? My husband and I have been trying for years to get him to date my cousin, who is in my sorority. He's always been too busy to take the time to date," she said accusingly.

"Before I met and fell in love with my Doug, I tried to get close to that Laurence," the woman named Keisha said cattily, leaning toward Miranda. "He didn't give me a chance to get close to him, the rascal. He always claimed he had too much work to date."

The woman who sat across from Jenny, named Beryl, stared at her, regarding her snootily. "How did you meet Laurence? In college?"

Jenny's mouth felt dry as cotton with all three of these women watching her. She gave them a tremulous smile. "I...I...well, I used to work for him."

"Oh, you're an architect," Miranda said, sounding impressed.

"No, no I'm not," Jenny said. "I was his secretary. When he returned home to Harper Falls and opened an office, I went to work for him a while." Suddenly, the room felt warmer to Jenny than it had before.

"Harper Falls," Keisha said, as though she were tasting something bitter. Furtively, she eyed her other friends at the table. "Laurence has spoken of his hometown. He said he had outgrown that little place."

Miranda said, "My husband told me that Laurence had to move home to look after his father,

who has been quite sick. He told me that Laurence
dreaded returning to this Harper Falls, but he was
obligated to do so. There's no one but him and his
father left now. His mother passed a few years ago,
you know," she informed both ladies, shaking her
head sympathetically.

"What college did you attend, Jenny? Miranda
and Beryl graduated Howard University. I graduated from Hampton U., which isn't too far from
Harper Falls," Keisha informed Jenny. "And we're
all sorority sisters." She beamed at her friends and
gazed back at Jenny, waiting for an answer.

Anxiety and shame consumed Jenny. She swallowed hard and managed to answer, "I...I haven't
gone to college...yet." She gave them a faltering
smile. "I married early. I have a daughter to raise.
No time or money for such a thing as college," she
said, laughing nervously. She hated herself for
revealing such personal details of her life to these
women whom she could never call friends.

Beryl blinked her eyes with incredulity at that
bit of information. "I certainly hope for Laurence's
sake that you are divorced." She laughed and so
did her friends. Jenny knew that she had intended
to be cruel and she felt wounded.

As the moderator for the evening began to
speak, Jenny was relieved. At least the interroga-
tion could rest for a while. The conversation died
down and Jenny directed her attention to the front

of the room. She spotted Laurence up front at the head table, sitting and looking handsome in his tux. He looked her way and smiled at her, warming her. Though Jenny had her back to the women, she could hear them chatting softly to one another. She was sure they were talking about her.

Jenny was pleased when that forty-five minute part of the program that Laurence had to participate in was over and he could rejoin her at the table. "Did you miss me?" he asked, touching Jenny on her bare shoulder.

The band began to play and couples made their way to the dance floor.

Laurence squeezed Jenny's chin affectionately. "Come on and dance with me, angel," he said, helping her out of her chair.

Jenny could feel the women watching her as she allowed Laurence to lead her away to dance.

As Laurence took her in his arms for a slow dance, he smiled down at her. "Are you enjoying yourself?"

Jenny wished she could tell him that she was, but she couldn't. "It's nice. But I feel out of place. Your friends reminded me that I don't belong."

Laurence glanced toward their table and glared. "I should never have left you alone with those vultures. Don't mind them. They would never like anyone I date anyway. Each one of them tried to squeeze her way into my life before she was married. And when they couldn't get me, they tried setting me up with a relative or a friend. I couldn't be with any of them. And you can see why. If I didn't consider myself a gentleman, I would tell you exactly what they are. Let's just say the word rhymes with switches." He laughed.

Jenny laughed, too. She totally agreed with his assessment of the women. The remainder of the evening, she and Laurence either danced, or he took her around the room to meet people who were more warm and friendly toward her.

As the evening drew to an end, Jenny excused herself to go to the restroom. While she was there, she heard the three women speaking in the lounge area of the ladies' room. They were smoking and gossiping about who had on what, and about the various infidelities of the men there. Touching up her make-up and hair, Jenny heard her name being spoken.

"And where the hell did Laurence Strong get that little nobody?" one of the women declared. "Help these men. They make me sick, going out of their social circle and getting these 'hood rats around us."

The other women grunted in approval.

"Oh, girl, you know the routine. They kill me, bringing some low class woman like this Jenny to our functions, trying to make them feel special, so that these kinds of women can keep making them feel super special behind closed doors. But we all know, when it comes time to settle down, men like Laurence Strong never marry the likes of someone as inadequate as this Jenny person. He's going to want someone who has class and is refined like we are." It was Miranda who had spoken.

"If you ask me, I think he's gotten what he deserves. Every time I look at the man, I think about that rumor that was going around about him," said one of the women. Jenny believed it was Beryl.

"What rumor?" the other two women asked in unison. "You've been holding out on us."

"Girl, my husband would have a coronary if I said anything. You know how these frat brothers are supposed to carry secrets to their graves. But I got my Mike to talk one night after too much wine and some great sex. Pillow talk," she said.

"Tell us about the rumor," Keisha said. "You can't tease us that way."

"I'd better not hear this again," the woman warned before continuing, "Laurence killed his brother."

The women could be heard gasping. Jenny's heart hammered from the disclosure.

"No, that can't be true. I mean, I know he can be an arrogant s.o.b., and quick-tempered on occasion. But I can't believe he's capable of killing anyone," Beryl said. Her shock could be heard in her voice.

"All of this happened when he was a teenager. It was said to be some kind of accident.

My husband clammed up when I wanted to know the details. I do know his older brother was the apple of his father's eye. Laurence left Harper Falls because of all the problems it caused in his family. He and his father haven't gotten along all these years, because of all the mystery surrounding the accident."

"Oh, girl, that is heavy," said Keisha. "Who would think a man as handsome and rich as he could do something like that?"

"It's a rumor. I don't know how much truth is tied to it," Miranda reminded the women cautiously. "So don't go repeating it."

"I know I won't," said one of the women. "It's an eye-opener. It really is."

Jenny heard other women entering the lounge area. They greeted the three women who had been talking alone and began a whole new conversation.

Jenny was humiliated by the things they had said about her. But to hear them reveal what they had about Laurence had completely alarmed her. Laurence had a dark side. She knew that. She wondered if it had really driven him to harm his older brother. She knew that he had spoken of his brother affectionately and with a bit of sadness. Yet she remembered that whenever she tried to get him to speak of what had caused his brother's death, Laurence would always become restless and choose to change the subject.

Keisha came into the restroom where Jenny was. She glanced at Jenny. For a moment, Keisha looked embarrassed at seeing Jenny. She gave Jenny a feigned smile, tossed back her hair in disdain and slipped into one of the stalls.

Jenny moved to the outer door, passing the other two women without looking their way. Fleeing, she heard them laugh and utter the words, "'hood rat." Normally that comment would have crushed her, but she decided that the unanswered questions about Laurence's past were of more concern to her.

It took everything in Jenny to gather her composure. However, she managed to greet Laurence, who had gotten their wraps while she was away, with a pleasant expression.

He greeted her with a warm smile. "It's started to snow," he informed her, helping her on with her wrap. "I have some fine brandy at my place. I can get a cozy fire going. It's a perfect time for lovers like us," he whispered in her ear.

Jenny gazed at the man she had fallen in love with and realized that once again she was toying with danger. If Laurence had been cruel enough to cause his own brother's death, what would he do to her if he lost control of his temper? The women had said that Laurence was young when this so-called accident had taken place. People make mistakes, she thought. Lord knows she certainly had. Where would she be had people held things she had done in her youth against her? she wondered.

Gazing into Laurence's face and finding his eyes twinkling with the mischief of his plans for the rest of the evening, she tried to banish her negative thoughts. This man who stood before her had no evil in his heart. She had detected sadness and loneliness, but certainly there was no violence, she convinced herself. Laurence had told her he loved her. But hadn't she believed the same thing about her ex-husband, Earl? Was she about to repeat the same mistakes in her life all over again, in the name of love?

Chapter 11

Later, at Laurence's condo, he and Jenny sat on oversized plush pillows in front of the fireplace. Laurence was disturbed by the reticent mood that Jenny had been in since they had left the dance. He had hoped that she would be in a much more amorous mood than she was. He leaned toward her and ran his fingers through her hair; he kissed the side of her face. "What's on your mind?"

She smiled weakly. She dared not question him right off about the questionable circumstances surrounding his brother's death. "I was thinking about something I overheard at the dance. The ladies were in the restroom and had quite a conversation about you and me."

He pulled her to him. "Come on, you're here with me. Don't even think about them anymore."

She held his hand to halt his eager touches. "I can't stop thinking about them or what they said."

"Tell me, what exactly was said? So we can put this behind us and get on with our evening." His voice was edged with impatience.

Her expression turned serious. "The ladies have a problem with you dating me. They have decided that you are seeing me for one reason only. Freaky sex. They called me a 'hood rat, Laurence. I heard them while I was in the restroom."

Laurence looked befuddled. "Hood rat? Exactly what is that?"

"It refers to a person who comes from a low income neighborhood. It's a way of saying that I don't belong. That I'm not good enough to be around people like yourself and them. That's what it means!" she exclaimed, jumping to her feet.

Laurence shot to his feet and went to her. "Those women have nothing to do with me or whom I choose to be with."

Jenny wanted to be convinced, but she wasn't. "Laurence, do you really think you and I could have any kind of life together? I mean, I really got to thinking, seeing you with your friends this evening. Before tonight, I dared to think that you and I could make a relationship work. Tonight was like holding a mirror up to myself and seeing myself in your world. I didn't like what I saw. Laurence, I'm not college-educated. I don't belong to one of those sororities like most of the women do. I don't have a designer wardrobe. I had to borrow clothes from Nina to go out. She had to show me how to coordinate all of this to look decent and..."

"Enough, Jenny," Laurence said curtly. He sighed then he gave her a tender look. "Have you ever considered that the reason I'm crazy about you is that you are different from anyone I've ever known? You're not some spoiled, pampered princess who has been handed everything on a silver platter. You're a hard-working woman who is raising an adorable, bright daughter. You're a woman who has survived the kind of things that would have destroyed some people. You're a fighter. And you're one of the prettiest, most sensual women I've ever known," he said in a soft tone. He enfolded her in his arms and kissed the top of her head.

Jenny's body betrayed her. She melted into the warmth of his body, wrapped her arms around his waist and gazed into his face. "You are some charmer."

"I'm more than a charmer. I'm full of honesty for my feelings for you," he said softly, placing a kiss beneath her earlobe and resting a hand on her breast.

Jenny removed his hand and attempted to walk away.

"Hey, where are you going?" He pulled her back to him. "I thought you and I were going to keep each other warm for the night." He placed layered kisses on her neck.

"Suppose I'm not interested?" she said, giving him a challenging look.

He gave her a puzzled look. "This is your last night in Chicago. Let's not spend it arguing over things that don't matter to me and shouldn't mat-

ter to you. You know how I feel about you. That's
all that should matter."

The remembrance of what had been said at the
dance weighed on her mind and in her heart. She
glared at Laurence. "Sex. It seems that the only
thing you and I really have in common is that.
We're basing our entire relationship on our physical attraction for one another. What other kind of
memories do we share together?" She began to
pace. "I've come clean and told you about my family. But you refuse to tell me anything about your
family and that brother of yours that you lost. You
haven't offered to take me to visit your father."

Laurence retained an affable demeanor, but
there was a distinct hardening in his eyes. "You're
wrong to think that way. I'm sorry that you do.
Every moment I've shared with you has been special. What's wrong with the physical attraction we
have for each other? It wouldn't be as good as it is
if you and I didn't care deeply for one another." He
stepped toward her and took hold of her. "Granted,
you and I haven't had the standard sweet romance.
But I'm prepared to give you the kind of love you
want, any way you want it." He leaned in for a kiss,
but she turned away.

"What is it that you want from me?" Laurence
asked. His voice was full of irritation.

She sighed and tried to gather her nerve to ven-
ture to the sensitive subject that troubled her more

than the personal attacks that had been made. "I happened to hear the women speak of your past. They made an insinuation about you and...and the cause of your brother's death."

At the mention of his brother, stress lines formed on Laurence's brow. "Exactly what did you hear? I want you to be honest with me," he demanded. He gritted his teeth.

Seeing him that way, Jenny realized she had set off his temper. She felt a cold fist close over her heart, but she knew she had to continue with what she had started. "There's...there's a rumor that you were responsible for his death. They made it sound as though you were jealous of him and wanted him out of the way."

All the warmth and admiration he had for Jenny faded from his face and was replaced by a scorching look. "And you believe that?"

"I...I don't want to," she said apologetically. "But you know my background. I can't trust anyone. I have a child to consider. I've seen you go into rages. I've witnessed your quick temper. I don't want to feel as though my life or my child's might be endangered because you can't control your anger." Tears welled up in her eyes. She knew that she had hurt Laurence by broaching the subject.

Laurence balled his fists and screwed his face into an incensed scowl. He stepped closer to her. "It's no use, is it? You still don't trust me. By now

you should know that I'm not the kind of man who
would abuse a woman or a child. How in the world
can you and I have a relationship if you're going to
believe everything you hear about me? There are a
lot of people in this town, and in the business that
I'm in, who would love to see me take a fall. They're
envious of where all of my hard work has placed
me. It's one of the reasons why I don't have many
friends," he fumed. "I thought you were different,
Jenny." He gave her an accusatory look.
"Obviously, I was wrong." He stared at her. "The
night is ruined," he said in a defeated tone. "I'll take
you back to Nina's."

Disconcerted by his refusal to defend himself,
she grabbed her wrap and slipped it on to leave. He
was right. Any attempt at a relationship was hopeless, if he couldn't share his past or something of
his family with her. Clearly she wasn't as important
as he had led her to believe she was. She cared for
Laurence. But she couldn't afford to be with a man
who had this cloud of violence in his past.

On the ride back to Nina's, Laurence was sullen
and didn't utter a word. The twenty-minute drive
seemed to take forever. As they pulled up in front
of the Wagners' building, Jenny turned to
Laurence. "There's no need for you to see me to the
door. I'll be just fine," she said. She hopped out of
his car and didn't bother to look back. Entering the
building, she told herself that it was over between

them. She felt the nauseating, sinking feeling of despair. Though it was over, she still loved him. She had no idea what she was going to do with all her leftover emotions. She was going to have to cry them out, she reasoned. Even though Laurence said he would never harm her or Chloe, she couldn't take the risk of allowing a man she even vaguely suspected of being abusive into her child's life.

Dressed in her nightshirt, Nina appeared in the hallway of the condo to greet Jenny.

"What are you doing back so early? I wasn't looking to see you until the morning. How was the affair?"

Jenny burst into tears.

Nina was at her side. "Jenny, my goodness. What happened?" She placed an arm around her friend's shoulder and led her toward the kitchen. "I'll fix us a hot drink, so we can talk."

Jenny settled at the kitchen table and placed her hands over her eyes. "I've made a mess of things. Laurence and I are through."

All the while Nina watched Jenny with a concerned look, she ran water into her tea kettle. "It might not be as bad as it seems. One argument doesn't end a relationship."

Jenny stared bleakly at her friend, revealing her agony. "I'm afraid this is more than an argument. I overheard something at the dance that bothered me. I questioned him. When I did, he flew off the handle. He accused me of not trusting him. And if I didn't trust him, I obviously didn't care for him, he claimed."

Nina took a seat in front of Jenny. "Oh, dear, Jenny. What was it that you overheard?"

Suddenly, Addison appeared in the kitchen, dressed in his sweats. "What's all the racket about? I was in the study working on an article. Did I hear crying? Is Chloe all right?" He stared at the two women. "Jenny, what are you doing home? I thought you and Laurence had plans."

Nina turned toward her husband. "Trouble, sweetheart."

Addison strolled over to the table, took a seat and studied Jenny's face. "What in the world has Laurence done to ruin the evening?"

"He didn't ruin the evening," Jenny said. "I did. I questioned him about his brother's death. I had overheard that he was responsible for his death."

"Jenny, no. How could you?" Addison asked in a harsh tone.

Nina gasped in shock at her husband's reaction. "Addison, please."

"I wish you had come to me with those allegations," Addison said, looking troubled. "Although his brother has been dead for nearly twenty years, Laurence still lives with the guilt of what happened. He didn't kill his brother. There's nothing like that in that man's heart. He was a teenager. He was driving the car that killed his brother. It was an awful accident."

Jenny was acutely embarrassed. She felt ashamed for assuming the worst. "Oh, no. I didn't know. Why would people call him a murderer?" She looked to Nina, then to Addison in dazed exasperation.

Addison's distinguished face had become brooding. "Because they are envious of Laurence and his success. People will say and do anything to hurt him. They have learned he's vulnerable to anything about his older brother, whom he had looked up to like a hero."

Jenny felt dreadful. Her eyes pooled with tears, thinking of the way she had doubted Laurence's character. If only she could take back her stupid question, the silly qualms she had had about him being yet another abuser in her life. "Why didn't he just tell me this?"

Addison met her horrified gaze. "It's a touchy, painful subject for him. He probably would have told you in time and in his own way, when he was ready to speak about it."

Nina touched Jenny's shoulder and squeezed in a caring manner. "Call him. Apologize. If he means anything to you, you must set it right."

"Yes...yes, you're right. I can't sleep, knowing that I have hurt him." Jenny jumped to her feet and started out of the room for a phone in another room. Then she froze in her steps and turned toward them with a helpless expression on her face. "It might be too late." Her voice broke.

Nina said, "You won't know that until you try to call him."

Jenny nodded and rushed to the other room to telephone. She dialed Laurence's number, but could only get his answering machine. A knot of anxiety constricted in her throat. She dialed several times during the night. She spoke to the blasted machine, urging him to call her. Finally she undressed, slipped into her robe and sat by the phone, waiting for the call that never came.

The next morning, Jenny and Chloe were due to take a noon flight back to Harper Falls. Jenny had slept restlessly, sitting upright on Nina's sofa. She had dressed before anyone in the house had gotten up. She took Nina's car and drove to Laurence's place. Since he hadn't returned her calls, she figured that maybe he would talk to her face to face.

On her second knock on his door, Laurence answered.

He stood before her, holding a glass of clear liquid with ice and looking muddled and disheveled. "What do you want?" he growled. His slurred speech revealed that he had been drinking. He scowled at her.

Her heart sank to see him in such a state. She was used to seeing him well-groomed at all times. "Laurence, I want to talk to you about..."

The telephone rang. Laurence left her with the door open.

She eased inside the house. She saw a nearly empty bottle of gin on the table in his living room, where he had entertained her the night before. His shoes, his tux coat and his tie lay on the floor in a cluttered heap.

Jenny stood in the middle of the living room, listening to Laurence talk on the phone in the kitchen. Since he hadn't invited her in and had failed to make her feel welcome, she dared not take a seat. She watched him from where she stood. He frowned, leaned his head back, then let it fall forward. His shoulders slumped. He muttered something into the phone, pulled it away from his ear and stared at it. His face drooped with sadness.

Sensing trouble, Jenny ventured toward Laurence. "Is there anything the matter?" she asked softly.

He straightened his shoulders and glowered in her direction as though he had forgotten that she was there. "Uh...it's my father. That was Jeremy. He was calling from the hospital. Jeremy had to rush him to the hospital. It's his heart. He's had a...a heart attack," he said, looking deflated.

Jenny stepped up to Laurence and placed her hand on his back. "I'm sorry, Laurence. Is there anything I can do for you?"

Laurence gazed at her like a sleepwalker; then his face crumpled. He enfolded her in his arms and began to sob.

Chapter 12

"Lie down on the sofa. Relax," Jenny encouraged Laurence in a gentle, caring tone.

Reluctantly, a distraught Laurence did as he was told.

Jenny was grateful that he did what she asked. This gave her time to settle her nerves. She had never seen a grown man cry. Arriving at his house, she had expected to be met with that arrogant attitude of his. Never in her wildest dreams had she imagined she would find him drunk. She wondered if her accusations had driven him to drink more than he should. Or had it been her decision to end their rocky relationship? She was certain that his tears had nothing to do with her. She knew that the fear of his losing his father, his only blood relative, was the reason for his emotional outburst.

While he rested, she prepared coffee to sober him. She kept an eye on him, sprawled on the sofa and looking defeated and hurt.

When the coffee was ready, she carried it to the living room, hoping to set him in a better frame of mind to face the crisis that waited for him in Harper Falls.

As she entered the room, Laurence sat up. "I feel like such a punk," he said, accepting the mug of coffee she offered him without meeting her gaze. "I haven't done that since…well, it's been a while." He hesitated pensively. "Jeremy told me that the doctor said that things don't look good at all." His voice was strained and low with emotion.

She took a seat near him. "There's nothing to be ashamed of. You have every right to be emotional," she said, touching his arm. "But you've got to be strong. You're no good to him in the condition you're in."

Looking dejected, he sipped on the hot coffee. "Jeremy told me that he found him a few hours ago, gasping for breath. His color was ashen. Thankfully, he called the paramedics right away. He gave me the number of his doctor. I should have called him at once to get the details. But I can't deal with the news yet."

Jenny listened patiently. She figured that was all that she could do for him at this time.

Laurence drank more of the coffee. "Before I came here to start my business right after graduate school, my old man and I had a terrible argument. I said a lot of things to him I had no right to say. Things I wish I had had the nerve to say right after the tragedy of losing my brother. My dad became a different man at that time. He was tortured because of Gary's death. He put my mother and me through hell. There was nothing that she or I could do to please or comfort him. He did straighten up when my mother threatened to leave him. But it didn't change his open disdain for me. The person he considered his son's murderer. Dad thought of Gary as his son, not Laurence's brother." Laurence's eyes glazed with sadness. He set aside his coffee and fell back in the chair. He rubbed his temples and closed his eyes.

Hearing his personal disclosure, Jenny's eyes brimmed with tears for Laurence's pain. True, she had wanted to know more of his life, but she had had no idea that he had so much grief, which he hid behind his arrogance and his aura of sophistication. If she had known this, she wouldn't have pushed him, or felt as though she had been denied some privileged information because he hadn't deemed her important enough to tell her. She wanted to go back to Nina's, so that Laurence could organize himself to leave for Harper Falls. But then she decided that he needed her, in the state he was in. Though most of the time Laurence acted confident and in control, even behaving like a bully at times, she could see now that he was just as insecure and afraid of life as she had been. Though he was rich and successful and she was a struggling single mother, they were both two lonely people who craved love and attention.

Never knowing her parents, Jenny had sought her affection and attention in all the wrong men. Fortunately for her, she had her daughter, Chloe, who kept her grounded and gave her unconditional love. Laurence, on the other hand, had no one but a father who had been emotionally abusive and had burdened him with the guilt of his brother's death. Yet, despite all the pain his father had given Laurence, Jenny could sense that he wanted to set things right with his father. She believed he needed to hear his father forgive him and to say he loved him. If this didn't happen, Jenny feared that Laurence wouldn't be able to move on with his life and live it with the kind of happiness he deserved.

Laurence leaned forward and placed his elbows on his knees. He stared at Jenny. Her face was scrubbed clean of make-up and her wavy hair was pulled onto the top of her head. Last evening she had been a sexy siren and today she reminded him of an angel. "What brought you back? I thought you never wanted to see me again." Secretly, he was glad that she had returned. He hated the way he had shut her out because she had questioned him about his past. She only wanted to know the truth, which she, of all people, had a right to know. Most of her life had been entangled with bullies and brutes. And he had scared her further with his occasional bad attitude and behavior.

Awkwardly, Jenny cleared her throat. "I came to apologize to you. I had a talk with Addison. He told me about the circumstances surrounding your brother's death." She touched his knee tenderly. "I'm sorry. That dance and those women set me off. They reminded me of what a misfit I was in that setting. I was out of my element, surrounded by all those beautiful and successful people. I was hurt, hearing the way those women talked about me. Then when I heard what they said about you, it only fed into my insecurities concerning you and me. I lashed out at you. I guess in my own way I wanted you to make me feel even worse about myself. But instead, I wound up hurting you more."

He remained expressionless. "Jenny, how could you be insecure about us? I've told you that I love you. Why couldn't you believe that?" he said impatiently. He jumped to his feet and began to pace.

"This is unimportant now," Jenny said, her voice taking on an edge. "You need to focus on your father," she chided softly.

"You're right," he agreed quickly. "I should call that doctor. I have flight plans to make and other things to organize at my office before I leave." He strode out of the room and into the kitchen. He grabbed the phone and made a call.

Watching him hovering over the phone with a notepad, his brow furrowed with preoccupation, Jenny got up and quietly left. She had made her apologies. There was nothing more to say at a time like this.

Just as Jenny made it to her car, she heard Laurence calling her. She turned to find him jogging toward her.

"I have arranged a noon flight back to Harper Falls. Isn't that the same flight you and Chloe are on?" He moved toward her and took her hand in his.

"It is," she said, squeezing his hand for comfort.

"Good. I want to be with you guys. I need..." His eyes glistened.

Seeing him emotional, she leaned into his chest. "We want to be with you, too. Let me help you pack. You can ride with me to Nina's. They can see us all off at the terminal."

Laurence gave her a smile of gratitude. He embraced her tightly.

She returned his embrace. She patted his back and gazed up at him. "As long as you need me, you can count on me," she assured him. Gazing into his face, Jenny saw a flood of relief. She assumed that her support at this time was the most important thing he had been given in quite some time. She wanted him to feel that with her he didn't have to be the superhuman man he had to be with everyone else. He could just be himself—Laurence Strong. A man who was just like any other man, with flaws and needs; a man who could admit that he was in pain and needed help.

***

Jenny was pleased that Chloe behaved herself as well as she did on the flight. She had taken her daughter aside and explained to the child that Laurence was troubled because of his father's illness. She told Chloe not to ask a lot of questions. She told the child that if she wanted to help Laurence, she was going to have to be as quiet as she could be. Chloe was concerned about Laurence. She kept watching him. Jenny was touched when her daughter reached out to the silent man and took his hand. Without saying a word, Chloe leaned her head against his shoulder. Laurence smiled at Chloe and touched her face gently. The sight made Jenny's heart swell with emotion. She had never been so proud of her little girl, who had shown such adult sympathy.

The moment they arrived at the air terminal, Laurence decided he should go straight to St. Luke's Hospital to see his father. Jenny agreed that it was the best thing to do. She and Chloe went with him, though she hadn't planned on visiting his father. She wanted to be with Laurence in case he needed someone to talk to, or to lean on for moral support.

Sitting in the waiting room of the hospital while Laurence visited his father, Jenny thought of how her life had changed. She thought of the number of times she had been in and out of the hospital as a battered woman. She remembered when she had to come all alone. That had been long before Nina had returned to Harper Falls. Jenny had forgotten the agony, the loneliness and the fear she had experienced. She had worried about Chloe, who was barely out of diapers when her husband started abusing her. That had been a lonely and hopeless time of her life. She knew she should leave her then-husband, Earl, but she hadn't had the courage or the presence of mind to do what she knew she must. Earl had brainwashed her and convinced her that she would be nothing without him, and that no other man would want her. Jenny cringed at the memory of how gullible she had been.

She placed an arm around Chloe's shoulder. The little girl napped quietly. Jenny placed a kiss on her daughter's forehead. She was thankful that she had Chloe in her life. She had been the inspiration Jenny needed to turn her life into something she could be proud of. She might not have the wealth or the success that Nina or Laurence had. But she worked hard and had dreams, which she was determined to make happen within the next few years.

After a while, Jenny saw Laurence shuffling toward her. Anxious to know what was going on with his father, she jumped to her feet and rushed to him. Her heart ached when she saw that Laurence's eyes were red-rimmed and saddened.

"How is he?" she asked, taking his hand and holding on to his arm.

Laurence sighed and cleared his throat. "I've seen him. It doesn't look good. The doctor said that there's been a lot of damage done to his heart. He's critical."

Jenny gripped his arm. "I'm sorry."

Laurence met her kind gaze. "I came for you and Chloe. I want the two of you to see too. You've been so kind to me by standing by me. I couldn't have faced this alone."

Jenny weighed his request. "But we're not your family. They won't let us in."

Laurence took her hand. "That's no problem. The doctor is a friend of Addison's. He told me that it was okay for me to bring you two along for a brief visit."

Jenny was touched that Laurence wanted her to be with him. She whirled away from him and went to awaken her daughter to take her to visit the ailing Mr. Strong.

On the ride in the elevator, Jenny ran her hand through her hair and fussed with Chloe's clothes. Although she knew Mr. Strong was very ill, she wanted to make a good impression. She wanted him to know that Laurence had a capable woman to care for and love his son.

When Laurence arrived at the Intensive Care Unit with Jenny and Chloe, the nurse gave him a questioning look.

"Dr. Riggs told me it was okay to bring my family to see my father," he told the nurse.

The nurse smiled and nodded her approval.

Arriving at Marvin Strong's room in the Intensive Care Unit, Laurence held Jenny's and Chloe's hands. The sight of his father hooked up to all kinds of medical equipment filled him with despair. There were so many things that the two of them hadn't resolved, he mused remorsefully. He released Jenny's and Chloe's hands and went to his father's bedside. He leaned down to him and kissed his forehead. "Dad, it's Laurence," he said in a soft, gentle voice. He fitted his hand into his father's lifeless one.

Marvin Strong's eyes fluttered open to meet his son's caring gaze. "Laurence," he muttered. "Sorry...I'm sorry...son."

Hearing his father's apology, and hearing him call him son as though he really loved him after all, erased all the anger and guilt Laurence had felt through the years. He palmed the side of his father's face and smiled, tears flowing from his eyes. "I love you, Dad."

His father's eyes fluttered and he attempted a weak smile. "And...I love you, too," he said in a measured tone.

Weeping softly from the reconciliation of father and son, Jenny hugged Chloe to her.

Laurence turned to her, held out his hand, and beckoned her to him.

"Dad, I want you to meet the two ladies who are important to me." Laurence positioned a stunned Jenny close to his father bedside. "Remember Jenny Martin, who was my secretary?" He lifted Chloe in his arms to give his father a better view. "And this is Chloe, her daughter." Jenny could only offer a cheerful smile to the man who was in such critical condition.

Laurence slid his arm around Jenny's waist. "I want Jenny to be my wife," he announced to his father, who struggled to focus on what his son was saying. "Will you marry me?" he asked, giving her a loving look.

Jenny's eyes watered even more. She said, "Yes. Yes I will." She rested her head on his chest.

Laurence kissed her briefly. He heard his father grunting and handed Chloe to Jenny, who stepped out of the way.

Marvin Strong lifted a trembling hand toward his son. "Be...be happy," he uttered.

Laurence gripped his father's hand and leaned over him to kiss his face. "I will," he said as tears streamed down his face.

His father took a deep breath and closed his eyes. The monitors started beeping an alarming sound and a nurse and doctor rushed into the room, ordering Laurence and his soon-to-be family out of the room.

Outside, huddled together in the hallway, an anguished Laurence and Jenny waited for the doctor.

After what seemed like forever, the somber doctor came for Laurence. "I'm sorry," he told him in a cool, professional tone. "He had suffered too much damage to his heart to survive."

Jenny held on to Laurence, who looked as though the sky had fallen on him.

He wept and hugged her tightly.

Sobbing with him, she returned his embrace and pressed her body to his to let him know that he had her love and was not alone.

Epilogue

A year later...

Sharing Thanksgiving Day with Nina and Addison, Jenny was amazed at how much her life had changed in a year. Last year she had been despondent over her relationship with Laurence and the job she had given up with him. A romance between them seemed hopeless.

Despite their rocky affair, she had dreamed of being Mrs. Strong. However, she had never imagined that it would be an eventuality.

After Laurence's father's death, they had returned to Chicago in February and gotten married on Valentine's Day. The wedding had been simple yet romantic. It had been followed by a week-long honeymoon in the Caribbean. There, she and Laurence had conceived the child that was due within the next few weeks.

Jenny stared at Nina, who cradled her infant daughter, Brandy Tyana, in her arms. Addison sat close to them, admiring his two loved ones. Jenny couldn't imagine them being any happier than she and Laurence.

Laurence entered the room from the hallway, carrying his camera. "Okay, it's time to take some pictures. We want to remember this first special day that our families have had a chance to celebrate." He snapped a picture of Nina and Addison with their daughter. Then he handed the camera to Addison. "You got to get a picture of me with my two favorite girls."

Addison hopped to his feet to oblige his friend. "Do you think we can get Jenny in the frame?" he asked, teasing her for how large her tummy had grown during the last months of her pregnancy.

Laurence reached over and affectionately rubbed Jenny's protruding stomach. "Don't mind him. You've never looked more beautiful." He winked at Jenny and turned to Addison. "Take the picture, man," he ordered, pulling Chloe close to his side.

Once Addison had snapped several pictures of them in various fun poses, Jenny insisted on taking a picture with Nina.

Nina took the sleeping Brandy and placed the baby in her carrier seat, which sat on a nearby table. She turned the seat so that the infant could be in the picture as well.

Jenny locked her arm with Nina's. "Everything has been so wonderful today. I couldn't be happier," she told the woman who had been like a sister to her. "Who'd ever think that you and I would end up with such wonderful husbands and such happy lives?" She was referring to their grim childhoods in foster care, and then her relationships with abusive men.

"God has had his hand on us." Nina squeezed her fingers. "Love and happiness becomes you. You're radiant." She slipped her arm around Jenny's shoulder and pressed her face to her friend's.

At that moment, Addison snapped a picture of them.

"We weren't ready," Jenny protested, rubbing her tummy. She felt mild cramps that reminded her of contractions. But that couldn't be now, she reasoned. She blamed the delicious meal—that, and the second servings she had eaten.

"I told him to snap it. It was perfect of you two, from where I was looking," Laurence said.

"Well, give us a chance to pose for another one," Nina ordered. "Let's pose in front of the fireplace, Jenny."

Jenny struggled out of her seat. As she stood, her water broke. The water ran down her legs. Jenny groaned and looked helplessly at her husband.

"Mommy, you peed on yourself," Chloe declared, covering her mouth with her hands and giggling.

"Laurence, looks like you're going to see that son of yours sooner than you thought," Nina said. "Jenny is going to have this baby tonight. Come on, we're going to have to get her to the hospital."

Addison rushed out of the room to get their coats. "Laurence, stop looking goofy, man. You're about to become a father. Marvin Gary Strong is ready to make his entrance into the world." Addison chuckled with delight over the name that Laurence and Jenny had chosen for the child, which the ultrasound had shown to be a boy. "Everything is going to be fine." He thrust Jenny's coat toward a nervous-looking Laurence. "Don't just stand there, man. Help your wife." Addison seemed to be getting a kick out of how the normally in-control Laurence had become speechless. He even took time to take a picture of him. "Nina will drive you guys to the hospital. I'll take my car and bring Brandy with me."

They all hustled to the car; Jenny settled into the backseat with Laurence sitting close beside her on one side and Chloe on the other; Laurence's arm was wrapped around her shoulder. "Are you all right?" he asked, looking at her as though she might give birth right then and there.

She took his hand and intertwined her fingers with his. "I couldn't be better." She rested her head on his shoulder. Tears misted her eyes. Her life was full of love with her husband, her daughter and the baby son that was soon to make its arrival into the world. It was unbelievable how far a lonely, lost girl like herself had come to find joy and happiness. Her husband kissed her tenderly. She tingled all over from the amazing love, and the life they now shared.

To order **Indigo Sensuous Love Stories**

or to receive a **Genesis Press** catalog,

call 1-888-463-4461

visit our website–www.genesis press.com,

or write to

**Genesis Press. Inc.
315 3rd Ave. N.
Columbus, MS 39701**

INDIGO: Sensuous Love Stories *Order Form*

Mail to:
Genesis Press, Inc.
315 3rd Avenue North
Columbus, MS 39701

Visit our website at

http://www.genesis-press.com

Name—————————————————————

Address—————————————————————

City/State/Zip—————————————————

1999 INDIGO TITLES

Qty	Title	Author	Price	Total
	Somebody's Someone	Sinclair LeBeau	$8.95	
	Interlude	Donna Hill	$8.95	
	The Price of Love	Beverly Clark	$8.95	
	Unconditional Love	Alicia Wiggins	$8.95	
	Mae's Promise	Melody Walcott	$8.95	
	Whispers in the Night	Dorothy Love	$8.95	
	No Regrets (paperback reprint)	Mildred Riley	$8.95	
	Kiss or Keep	D.Y. Phillips	$8.95	
	Naked Soul (paperback reprint)	Gwynne Forster	$8.95	
	Pride and Joi (paperback Reprint)	Gay G. Gunn	$8.95	
	A Love to Cherish (paperback reprint)	Beverly Clark	$8.95	
	Caught in a Trap	Andree Jackson	$8.95	
	Truly Inseparable (paperback reprint)	Wanda Thomas	$8.95	
	A Lighter Shade of Brown	Vicki Andrews	$8.95	
	Cajun Heat	Charlene Berry	$8.95	

**Use this order form
or call:
1-888-INDIGO1**
(1-888-463-4461)

TOTAL _____
Shipping & Handling _____
(\$3.00 first book \$1.00 each additional book)

TOTAL Amount Enclosed _____
MS Residents add 7% sales tax

INDIGO *Backlist Titles*

QTY	TITLE	AUTHOR	PRICE	TOTAL
	A Love to Cherish	Beverly Clark	$15.95 HC*	
	Again My Love	Kayla Perrin	$10.95	
	Breeze	Robin Hampton	$10.95	
	Careless Whispers	Rochelle Alers	$8.95	
	Dark Embrace	Crystal Wilson Harris	$8.95	
	Dark Storm Rising	Chinelu Moore	$10.95	
	Entwined Destinies	Elsie B. Washington	$4.99	
	Everlastin' Love	Gay G. Gunn	$10.95	
	Gentle Yearning	Rochelle Alers	$10.95	
	Glory of Love	Sinclair LeBeau	$10.95	
	Indiscretions	Donna Hill	$8.95	
	Love Always	Mildred E. Riley	$10.95	
	Love Unveiled	Gloria Green	$10.95	
	Love's Deception	Charlene A. Berry	$10.95	
	Midnight Peril	Vicki Andrews	$10.95	
	Naked Soul	Gwynne Forster	$15.95 HC*	
	No Regrets	Mildred E. Riley	$15.95 HC*	
	Nowhere to Run	Gay G. Gunn	$10.95	
	Passion	T.T. Henderson	$10.95	
	Pride and Joi	Gay G. Gunn	$15.95 HC*	
	Quiet Storm	Donna Hill	$10.95	
	Reckless Surrender	Rochelle Alers	$6.95	
	Rooms of the Heart	Donna Hill	$8.95	
	Shades of Desire	Monica White	$8.95	
	Truly Inseparable	Mildred Y. Thomas	$15.95 HC*	
	Whispers in the Sand	LaFlorya Gauthier	$10.95	
	Yesterday is Gone	Beverly Clark	$10.95	

* indicates Hard Cover

Total for Books _____
Shipping and Handling_____
($3.00 first book $1.00 each additional book)